ROOTS RUN DEEP

J. KRAWCZYK

Ghoulish Ghosts
an imprint of Ghoulish Books & Little Ghosts Books
San Antonio, Texas | Toronto, Ontario

ISBN: 978-1-963801-07-1

www.GhoulishGhosts.com

Cover by Chris Krawczyk

THE LAUNDRY ROOM

I WISH SHE had said anything else before she died. I'd even prefer, 'I regret everything.' Every breath since has replayed her last words.

It gnaws at me. Incessant. All consuming.

I've tried to sleep in the hospital, but as soon as I drift off, those words replay. I think I could sleep if she had said anything else. I knew what was coming. Who could rest and also prepare themself for the inevitable? Her memories aren't her anymore. Her body is. It's only been a day, but all I know is that my wife is dead.

Fifty-three years of marriage and my entire life is forty-nine hours long.

I couldn't find an excuse to stay in the hospital for another night. Maybe I should have stayed in a motel. This house has never been without her. It seems larger somehow. A place that once comforted me now feels like a prison of open space. Corners are frightening. Doors lead to a void. I don't want to move. Around each bend, I'll just find another area that I no longer know.

Oh my. It's been a while since I've seen myself.

The mirror behind the door in the laundry room surprises me. I avert my eyes to avoid seeing her coats but see myself instead. I've somehow lost and gained weight. My neck seems longer than I remember and my shoulders, now hunched forward, seem to melt lugubriously down into my frail hips. My flannel pants fan out like a wrinkled Christmas tree. I don't bother tucking in my shirt anymore.

Selfish instincts want to blame the recent loss, but I've been like this for quite some time. What happened? This body no longer holds a purpose. It can't provide. It can only take. Less than useless. It's a shame so foul that I find myself disgusted with my own body and mind.

Once a monument to cleanliness, this room has eroded into a wasteland of cloth. All mine. Clean, yes, but abandoned. I've been rotating four shirts and two pants for almost a decade. I'm not sure why. They still fit.

It happened the day after she did a cycle, so her clothes were sorted into her dressers or hung on wooden hangers. Those hangers used to be my alarm clock on the weekends. I'm not sure how the rustling of a human body kept me asleep, but their hollow wooden jostling stirred me awake. I'm not sleeping in our bedroom tonight. Most likely, ever.

Why did I let her cater to me so? Little by little, my participation atrophied until she made every meal and tended to every plant in the garden.

The garden.

There's a cushioned bench out back. I could sleep outside tonight. The laundry room leads into our backyard, so I don't have to confront the rest of the house. I find a limp throw blanket. It's a gift from a relative who I can't recall for a holiday that I can't remember. It's foreign enough to let me use it. That's all I need. The backdoor isn't locked. How long hasn't it been locked?

I step into a wall of stagnant cool air. The time of day is disorienting. It's that sliver of time when it's not yet morning but too close to dawn to be considered night. Thank the heavens for covering itself. The cloud cover is thick enough to conceal the full moon, let alone starlight. Good. It better do the same with the sun. I could live without ever seeing the sun again.

Oh my. The garden.

It's still tidy, but organic; an organized mess. Just what she aimed for while bleeding into our untempered acreage. An oasis of gentle life encased in a sarcophagus of mountainous pine and barbed thicket. It has never felt isolating until now. With the endless blanket of clouds above, vertigo strikes my gut. It wrenches into my hips, and physical pain carves its way down my legs. Air exhales from my lungs as if I were punched in the solar plexus, and the returning air meets a brick wall in the back of my throat.

How did the dirt rise to meet me? Did someone hurl a clump of earth into my face? My nose tingles, and I see flickers of dancing light that I know aren't there. I reach up to rub my eyes, but my hands meet more dirt. Panic grips my spine and pulls my stomach against the earth. If I could breathe, I'd be hyperventilating.

Is this what I've scoffed at my entire life? Is this *that aliment* reserved for the weak-willed hypochondriacs? Am I having a panic attack?

It hurts. How does it hurt? Isn't this psychosomatic? My nerves are splitting apart; a migraine thrashing to escape the confines of my skull; a cerebral coup invading my body through agony. A lifetime of apologies rage through my joints as they burst into acid. I can't move. I can't even think. Somebody. Something. Save me from this.

Then my eyes find them.

The soft fog of my vision recognizes the shapes. They fine-tune and gradually find hard edges as my throat clears a path to breathe. My lungs force the air down, gradually blazing a cavity of space inside my chest. A rhythm returns to my breath as my hands grasp the soil. My legs writhe as they remember how to move. Sensations other than torment return to my fingers and toes, and relief emanates through my appendages. My hips and shoulders slack, and I flop flat back on the ground. This is somewhat reminiscent of that moment after you vomit. That euphoric awe when nausea is vacuumed out of your soul. You can instantly exist again. Relief. It puts everything into immediate perspective. I am grateful to no longer be betrayed by my body.

Rocks. My saving grace was a pile of rocks. They're propped against our wood-warped toolshed; black rubber tubing, various gardening tools. She finished collecting the rocks and purchased the remaining materials to build a pond. I have to embrace my soothing beacon. I push myself off the ground and shamble my way toward the shed. The spasm removed my knee's joints, so I lumber with rods for legs and a weary disposition. It's hard to gauge if I'm actually in pain or if I'm in fear of pain.

She talked about a pond for years, but maintaining the garden, the house and myself, stole time away from her actual wishes. What a selfish putz I've become. All we have is time, and I took more than my own. What have I really been doing? It's hard to imagine looking back. Re-reading books and re-watching shows I've absorbed so many times over I can recite them from memory. How is that a way to live? How many poems were written about the sanctities of retreading your past? I guess that makes me bad at being human.

Oh my, would you look at that? I'm taller than I thought.

It appears the spasms from my cerebral rebellion dug a fairly decent hole in the dirt. I did not think my body was capable of making that much of an impact on the ground. My heels dug into a foot of hard soil and sand. I was able to contort my spine in ways that would dig that wide of a hole. And I'm fine. Every joint survived.

I could probably fix things around the house that I believed I couldn't. I could probably go up the attic stairs myself. I could probably change the oil in the car myself. I could probably start and finish that pond that Alex—

There was a second. No longer than a glance. I didn't think about it. I didn't think about you dying. Or that you're dead. Or that every single second I have left on earth is without you. It was elating. Something I didn't think was possible. How did I do it?

My eyes find the pile of rocks before my brain does.

Listen. Listen to your body. Let it wander and give it what it needs. Whether to nurture mourning or avoid it, I will follow your lead.

I'm always surprised by the hollow feel of the wooden handles of gardening equipment. Almost weightless. It's not until the weight of the steel shovel transfers into my grip that the rest of my body follows suit. My first few steps drag the spade behind me, but the shame of my transgressions lobs the collar into my free hand. The soil is soft from my agony, and the blade cuts through the ground with little assistance from my own weight. All I have to do is dig. I'm not even aware of where I'm displacing the dirt. All I have to focus on is digging. That's all. Dig deep. Dig wide. Then, place in the liner, followed by the pipes, filter, and skimmer.

That's when it starts to take shape. I can lay the fountain of rocks, gravel, and flora. Maybe I can transfer a few of the more amphibious plants from the garden. There's plenty of cattail and sweet flag grass. The zebra-striped bamboo can encase the pond as a whole. An oasis within an oasis. We don't have much in terms of lilies or duckweed. That'll be something I'll have to purchase. We'll have to forgo fish. There are too many birds of prey to support—wait, what?

That can't possibly be a root. Feels like my shovel hit a metal beam. There's no give whatsoever. How silly of me. Just because I can't pierce a sturdy root doesn't mean there's reinforced structural steel under our garden. Either way, I'm far too deep to start over. As I step into the hole, I just now realize I'm barefoot. When did I take my boots off? I remember taking them off in the hospital. Did I drive home without shoes?

I find where the root ends, and it's right in the center of our pond. It's not horrendously thick, either, as it's less than a foot wide. I can do it. In just an hour, I've already proven myself more than capable. I can split this root with sheer will. With the full arch of my back and hands over my head, I bring the shovel down. The impact shivers through my limber muscles and reinforced joints. What else can I do? I raise the shovel as many times as I need. My body craves more, and I yield to its whims. Dirt cascades into the air as I exhale from tireless lungs. I can taste the salt of my sweat on the corner of my lips. Of all the days I've had, this is the one I can defy myself. I don't care if it is industrial metal embedded in our garden. I shall sheer it apart. If I can do this, then maybe I can go on. Maybe I can live another day without her. And then another. And then another. Just like how this shovel can keep coming down.

"Ah, fucking hell!"

I spring backward. General aches, flimsy joints, and reality unceremoniously return to my person. The facade of invincibility evaporates, as does my inflated pride.

"Hello?"

It's stupid to think there would be a response, but I don't know what to do. I would prod the root with the shovel, but I dropped it, and my raucous shoveling made my body stiff. I'm also afraid to move, because if I do, will that root move again?

It was too deliberate. It raised up from the ground, writhed like a snake, and then rested back on the ground. It looked animatronic. It wasn't brief or subtle enough for me to argue a trick of the mind. It happened. Did I hurt it?

"Hey."

No response.

"HEY!"

I feel ridiculous. I'm yelling at dirt. I know what I saw. But then again, what did I see? This thing's caked in dirt, and I'm tired, stressed, and traumatized. I nudge it with my bare foot. Nothing. I test my knees as I kneel down. They're not as taught as I expected. Do I allow myself to believe in pain to avoid labor? I must. I've doubled my range of motion in the last hour just by trying.

It feels like a root. My first few prods are brief; I'm

acting as if it could bite. It remains lifeless in the dirt. With the lack of fangs, I brush away the compacted soil. Black. So much so that its lack of color pierces through the night-soaked earth. As dark as pitch, it's as if I could dip my hand into its void. But it's solid. Harder than bark and seemingly petrified. Maybe it is man-made. A cable, perhaps? No, it has a base that has thin roots that branch out further into our garden.

I remove more clumps to find what I assume are bulbous growths. They're not. They're something else. Whatever this is, its scales are symmetrical and curve into fine points. The details are hard to perceive, given its particular intense shade of black. It's bizarre. Closer to a crustacean than a plant. But when it moved, it slithered. How could it do that with such a coarse bark plating? Like marble.

It mustn't have moved. Trick of the mind. I have to stop this and come to terms with my reality. I'm three feet in the ground, digging out a long-abandoned electrical cable.

Exhaustion has taken its toll, and I'm prone to discrediting myself. This workday isn't too long; I just lack ambition. This math actually checks out; I'm just stupid. I'm not actually sick; I'm just lazy. Then I steamroll through an actual sickness, and I'm worse for the wear. Why can't you similarly gaslight your own reality? Maybe it's a cue to stop what I'm doing. I'm avoiding grief when I should be soaking in it. Please just go inside, take a shower, and cry in our bed. I'll eventually fall asleep, and when I wake up, take it one step at a time. I can learn to be again. I can—

"Ah hell—what!?!"

The root opened its mouth and gasped.

It's still in my hand, and now I'm afraid to let it go. You wouldn't loosen your grip on a poisonous snake. It's breathing through a serrated, gaping mouth and pink, sinewy throat.

Those aren't tumors but features of a callous face.
"Oh my, oh my, oh my, oh my . . . ."
It's suffering. At least, that's what it looks like. It's at my mercy. I look down at this brittle thing and only one image pierces through my mind. Even under all of her tubes and monitors, I could make out the words Alex was gurgling through her oxygen mask. Her last words. It's the same faint plea. This creature is pleading with that same sentiment. Even though this thing can't speak, I hear her same muffled, "*help me.*"

THE KITCHEN

OH MY. When did the sun come up?

It's been quite some time since I've felt this limber and energized, and I didn't even sleep. My eyes have been on the ground for so long that I missed the night's transformation into blue.

It's there. Exhaustion. I'm banking it. I'll pay that debt later. My consciousness is on an exclusive diet of whatever emergency hormones I have left. I know it's unsustainable, but there's work to be done.

We match now. I'm covered in just as much dirt as my friend. However, as it's much longer than its diminutive face suggested, it's still buried in earth. Its root system is much more complex than I assumed as well. I've counted eighty-seven offshoots of thin black branches. Each foot of liberation is met with a jostle, and each jostle softens more dirt for me to dig. It stretches into its newly acquired empty space and, with an eyeless face, watches me exhume it further. I don't know how much bigger this thing can possibly be. It might actually creep off our property and into the forest.

All I know is the sun is up, so I can drink something other than water.

We've been taking water breaks. It doesn't seem to have a throat, but I see a series of sinewy veins that I can't identify as flesh or plant. Either way, it seems to request a spray bottle of fresh water around the same time I find myself needing a drink. I hope water from a spigot is okay.

I get a zing of childhood nostalgia, but I'm sure that bias doesn't translate. I try not to drink caffeine past noon, but I've been awake for thirty-six hours, and it doesn't look like I'll be sleeping in the next twelve. It needs my help.

Is this the first time I've been in the house since I found our guest? Or are we its guests? We've been here forty-eight years, but that's a heartbeat to a tree. But it's not a tree, is it? Maybe an animal that's camouflaging as a root system. Something undiscovered; something massive and underground. There's that fungus in Oregon that is over two-thousand acres. Maybe it's a more animate fungus. Doesn't explain the root system. Details to explore for later.

I'm going to keep my kitchen visit curt. I'm still not prepared to live in our house. Soon. Maybe. This project seems to be the distraction I need. If we're lucky, freeing that thing will tire me out until grief and sleep coalesce. But not right now—

"Excuse me, hello?" A thin voice calls from the front foyer.

The front door is slightly ajar. It takes a second for me to realize this, but there's a sliver of refracted light on my discarded boots.

Oh, that's where I left them.

"Yes?" Hello?" My words are kind, but my voice is callous. My hand gets to the door before she has a chance to open it any further.

"Oh, hello, uh, sir. Is this the Carver residence?" A gentle, round face asks through the crack in the door.

"It is."

"Um, are you Mr. Carver? Edward Carver?"

"It also is."

"Um, first, uh, my condolences on your recent loss."

"Thank you, but I'm busy at this time. Can you—"

"I'm the pathologist assistant at Mercy Regional Hospital. We've been trying to reach you."

"Like I said, I'm bu . . . " What could possibly be more important? "Please, come on in."

I ease my nerves as I step away from the door.

"Thank you. Shoes off?" She asks.

"If you don't mind." The irony in this is that my bare feet are filthy. Hopefully, I can distract her with, "Coffee?"

"If you're having a cup," she responds as she notes my dirt-laced bare feet and the subsequent trail of soil to the backyard. I catch an anxious nod of recognition before she takes her shoes off next to mine.

"Only if that cup can be a mug." My hand instinctively flinches and reels back from the light switch. I don't want to see the kitchen yet. We're the lone house in a cul-de-sac encased in greenery and bark. You don't get here by accident or live here without getting your hands dirty. Earthy mitts are the norm, but a kitchen unkempt enough to sustain non-human life can raise an eyebrow.

"Oh yeah, that's fine, thank you. But just a splash. I'm a cheap date when it comes to caffeine."

I didn't hear most of her response, but the word caffeine snaps me out of my trance. I guess the word association puts my focus back on track. I flick on the kitchen light yet keep my eyes on our guest. Whatever I have to do to get through this without having her discover the project in our backyard.

"I have to grind some beans, so please forgive the time and noise."

It's much cleaner than I expected. We ate out two nights in a row before I found her, so I guess the kitchen hasn't had the chance to get cluttered. The aqua tile countertop pops through the metal sheen of the sink and the beechwood cabinets. This time of day is optimal for the kitchen. These colors and textures deserve morning sunlight. Now, that tender coziness feels spiteful without her. A reminder of a sense of security I'll never feel again. I want to be able to revel in it, but the only emotions available are envy and bitterness. There's a creature beyond comprehension outback, and my wife just died. I'll run on autopilot for now.

Oh my, we have so much coffee left. Good. One less cog to clutter my flaming Rube Goldberg machine of a brain. I pour the coffee beans into the grinder.

"Brace your ears."

My human guest does a mousy nod as she shrugs her shoulders. She eases her shoulders as the grinder dies, and I fill the kettle.

"I'm sorry, but I didn't get your name?"

"I guess not. Mia. I'm Mia."

"Morning, Mia."

"Morning, Edward."

"Cream? Sugar?"

"No, thank you," Mia responds. She can somehow stand comfortably nervous. It might be her oversized cardigan, stressed jeans, and laceless beige sneakers, but she looks like she designed her aesthetic after a childhood pillow. She also came here after a shift at a hospital's morgue, so she probably earned that leisure suit. It makes the wait for boiling water bearable. Well, right before boiling. I lift the kettle off the burner.

Oh my, that smell.

A once-rote comfort is now a foreign pin prick. Just keep making coffee. Stay despondent and watch your hands do the work. I abandon waiting and immediately press the grounds through the hot water. All I yearn to do, as I prepare the coffee, is return to our creature. It awarded me with a few fleeting moments of oblivion, and I must repay that kindness. In the meantime . . .

"Here we are." I clink Mia's mug on the kitchen island as I cradle my own. "Please, feel free to sit."

"Oh, thanks. Been on my feet all day, and driving isn't exactly relaxing, I know you're sitting down, but it still takes up brain space," Mia remarks as she nestles into our wooden bar stool.

"I used to do a bread route, so I know what you mean."

"Whoa, what were those hours like?"

"Alarm went off at two, and I went to bed at six."

"Oof, I hear they pay well, though."

"It put me through college so I could eventually return to the bread route."

"That lucrative, huh?"

"That and people don't make sandwiches out of fine art diplomas," I add as I take my first sip of coffee. Oh my, it's so nice. It's like drinking a knitted sweater. Everything about it is soothing, from the smell to the porcelain warmth in my hands. It also reminds me of something vital.

I should eat. It's been over two days.

"Um, so I'm sorry again for disturbing you at such a sensitive time, but there are affairs that need addressing."

"Funerals and whatnot?"

"Unfortunately, yes."

"Just mail me her ashes and tack it on my bill."

"Was it her wish not to have a service?"

"We don't have children, and we outlived most of our friends and family. The ones that are still kicking have devolved into republicans." Except for maybe Derek. I should give Derek a call.

"Oh . . . okay. I'm sorry to hear that," Mia responds, avoiding a sip of her knitted sweater.

"It was actually our ideal lifestyle."

"So a direct cremation is what you're looking for?" Mia takes out a yellow notepad from somewhere in her cardigan. She scribbles our name down and then 'DC.'

"Suppose."

"Okay, but you'll still need a funeral home for the body to rest until the death certificate and cremation permit come through, however."

"There isn't a furnace at the hospital?"

"Not for human remains."

"Hm . . . remains." My mind goes blank, and my mug becomes two hundred pounds.

"Um, I'm sorry. I'm sorry. That was rude of me," Mia says as she puts her pad back into her cavernous cardigan. She contemplates taking a sip of coffee but merely nestles it in her hands. For such soft and sheepish body language, her hands are rough like that of a deep-sea fisherman. Sinewy and coarse with gnawed, chipped nails. I envy them; mine have withered away to skin and bone.

Hopefully, I can change that.

"It's okay." I sip my coffee and time unfreezes.

"I'll report your wishes to the hospital and see what's available for your spouse. Is it okay if I stop by tomorrow around the same time with paperwork that requires your signature?"

"That's fine." No, it's not.

"Okay then. I'm going to stop taking up your time and try to fall asleep after the coffee."

"Oh, I'm sorry. I could've done a tea."

"No regrets," Mia says, knocking back the rest of her coffee. "But maybe tomorrow."

"Sounds like a plan."

I round the kitchen island and walk with her to the front door. She says something again about mourning, but I'm barely paying attention. Knowing that her stay is ending has emboldened my ambitions to continue digging.

"I'll see you tomorrow."

"Thank—" I close the door before I finish the "you."

I'll need a refill of coffee before I return to my excavation. I leave the French press resting beside the burner while I clean up the grounds. I'd love to recapture that porcelain heat.

What is that?

I use a sponge to wipe up some residual coffee on the tile, but something darker than the coffee emerges from where the counter meets the wall: a pitch vine has grown through brittle cement. It's only a few inches in length, and not only has it invaded our home, but it has also budded flowers.

THE GARAGE

OH MY.

This could be a problem.

My memory says otherwise, but I'm looking at more brittle particle boards than gardening tools. The vacant hooks clinging to splintered pegs outnumber the equipment, so my memory may not be totally unfounded. It's hard. The older you get, the less space you have. There are large swaths of life that feel so weak it's like they never happened. How much of my time does that account for? I bet the majority. It's not like we log each time we drink water or go to the bathroom. There's only so much room.

Eventually, significant interactions get lumped in with the mundane.

There are faint flickers of me handing over tools to friends, but I have to excavate them from wherever it is that neglected experiences go to fade away. It is exhausting. Like doing complex math without the aid of a pen and paper. Images so starved of details that they may as well be imaginary. Did the sights and smells of our garage spark something that happened or build something that could have happened?

I don't know and have no way of knowing now.

The creature in the garden requires tools beyond what I have. It's larger than what I've presumed. Its central root is as wide as I am tall, and it extends under our shed. It most likely goes into the forest. As intimidating as that prospect may be, what really concerns me is its depth. Its offshoots take up the entirety of the garden and most likely our property, but they all continue downward. I've dug through as much soil and clay as my body will allow, but the deeper I go, the denser and more riddled with stone the earth becomes. The beast's roots run deeper still and I continue to dig.

With each inch of liberation, the creature gyrates its limbs. It disrupts the soil just enough to soften it for me. That's impressive. Most of the soil contains dense volcanic sediments. Like digging through building rubble. So, the idea that it can move and grow through that is as mystifying as terrifying.

Andisols, I think. Something like that. It starts with an 'A.'

Maybe that's what it is: some kind of giant, clonal organism spawning from ash. Its color is that of obsidian, and it feels more like slate than wood. That means it's old. Primordial. But then why does it seem to have flesh? Or a mouth?

I truly cherish that one of the most significant discoveries in human history is in my backyard. That it needs *my* help. Not a boardroom of scientists motivated by a boardroom of politicians motivated by a boardroom of CEOs.

Even without eyes, it watches me. I can't detect malicious intent, but how the hell do you detect anything from something unimaginable? It knows what I'm doing. It knows I'm trying to help. It needs me, and I need it, and that's how it'll be.

I'm avoiding the big roadblocks. Do I knock down our shed? I believe I do, but I need to move the debris. I can rent an excavator. One of those mini ones. That way, I can knock down the shed, move the remnants, and continue to dig. What if it's deeper than what the backhoe can allow? Then, I'd need to dig a slope for the excavator to get into the ground. I'd have to pile the dirt somewhere on our property. I'd essentially destroy our garden. Ruin our house. Our home. There's no way. That can't be worth it. But what if it's that big? I can't leave it entombed in our backyard.

My phone's been dead for hours, maybe days. I'm not even sure why I check if it has power. It can only be dead. Time's becoming a swamp of endless evenings. Without the luxury of a routine, it's hard to differentiate the days. It feels silly to consider something a new day when you haven't slept. This whole ordeal has been a single day. One unwieldy, sixty-hour day.

Hmm.

Ordeal.

I'd be ashamed of myself for using such a tame word, but I'm too tired to think of a better one. I'll collapse eventually. Until then, let's see if I can rent an excavator.

There's an outlet I use to charge my phone near the workbench. At first, I can't remember the last project I was working on, but then, it strikes me. As soon as my fingertips touch the stainless steel mesh, I remember. I was working on a chiminea; just like everything else in here, it's coated in dust.

I used to make things. I used to like making things; getting inspired inside hardware stores was a highlight of my life. Seeing a desk or a lamp or a chiminea and telling myself, 'I could build that' would ensnare my ambitions for weeks. It was intoxicating. Stronger than any drug I've tried.

We missed sitting out back in the winter, and I was going to change that. The chiminea was going to have a face, and the mouth was going to house firewood. There's that fine arts degree. Well, now I have a new project. I won't stop until that creature is free, just like I didn't stop until there was a desk, a lamp, or a sh-

My phone's back on, and I've missed a few dozen calls. Among the flood of nameless missed calls from the hospital, one red 'Derek' slips through the cluster of numbers. His accompanying texts make me want to turn my phone back off. I don't read them, but his last alert starts with, 'Hey, you alright? I was-'

No. No, I'm not alright. But thank you, Derek. I'll get back to you. I don't know when. I can't even fathom a time when I'd be in the right headspace to call you back. It doesn't seem possible. But you know what does?

"Hi there, I'm interested in renting one of your backhoes . . . mini, please . . . A week, maybe two . . . today if possible . . . oh, yes, I suppose it is . . . "

When did the sun go down?

"Tomorrow will be fine . . . thank you . . . okay. That's fine . . . I'll do that right after I hang up. Carver. Edward Carver. You spell it just like you imagine . . . Yup, as if you were the person carving the turkey . . . how much? . . . of course . . . okay, this number works . . . thank you. Take care."

They'll text me a form for my banking information and address, and they'll get to it. Didn't even ask if I could drive it. I'm sure it's intuitive. How much damage could I possibly do by myself?

"Excuse me, sir?"

A frail voice with a South American accent seeps into our space.

Oh my, how long has he been standing there? A silhouette stands in the center of our open garage door. I can't make out many details, but he's a shroud of a man, hopefully in a trench coat and flat cap hat. We live down a series of winding roads and are engulfed by trees. I know I'm tired, but I should have at least heard his car or seen his headlights. The only vehicle I can see behind him is our own.

"Pardon me, who are you?"

"Forgive my intrusion, I'm—"

He attempts to enter our garage, but I can't have that.

"Please, stay where you are."

"Certainly. Apologies."

He's a priest. The stuttering steps he took before

receding into the darkness gave me a glimpse of his face. The first thing I spotted was the white collar. He's also pale. Young, pale, and with a goatee as thin as his voice.

"Sorry, Father, you startled me."

"Rightly so, rightly so. I am here uninvited." He takes off his hat and holds it close to his torso, nervously rotating it counterclockwise in the slightest of increments. The whole action seems to lock into place, hunched over the hat in his hands, looking up through his brow on a crooked neck. The posture of a vulture.

"You certainly are. How can I help you?" I step into the center of the garage to establish a line of entry. You can come in, but not past me. He does. That is some impressive hair for a paperboy cap to cover. Defying gravity and growing upward in a tangled black nest of thick ringlets. His wool coat and cap is kissed with moisture. It's not a downpour, but it's raining in a haze that gradually zigzags the droplets. I go to grab a paper towel from my desk dispenser, but only the cardboard roll remains.

"Sorry, hold on." I find the closest washcloth near me. Giving it a quick inspection, I toss it to find a cleaner washcloth on the other side of the garage. So much for that line of entry.

"Obliged," the man says as he takes the daisy-embroidered rag. "I would have knocked, but I saw the garage light and your dancing shadow within."

I'm not sure if it's because English is his second language or he's a young priest, but it sounds like he learned the language by reading tales from the crypt.

"I'm sorry. I haven't been checking my phone. It's been a distracting few days," I say.

"I'm sure it has, but I'm also sure 'distracting' is an unworthy word for your predicament?"

"Just as unworthy as 'predicament.'"

"Yes, well, rightly so, my friend, rightly so."

"Hm, 'friend.'"

"Indeed, sir. Indeed. I'm here to hopefully add solace

to your new reality. To let you know it is not the end of the world. How are your faculties under recent circumstances?"

"Oh my, um, how do you answer that? There's nothing to compare this to."

"It's not for the faint of heart." He dabs the washcloth on the nape of his neck and reveals what seems to be the end of a much larger and hidden tattoo. Black wisps of pointed ends. I bet it's reminiscent of stained glass. It has that same rigged art style.

"No, it is not."

"Wish it wasn't you, I'm sure."

"Well, yes and no. As horrendous as this is, I'm glad I got to be there for her. She doesn't have to go through this part. Being without her . . . or me, I suppose. Treading water until the earth takes me."

"Yes . . . well . . . There is no right way to grieve, but there are plenty of wrong ways . . . "

The priest is quiet, seems incapable of looking me in the eyes. I guess that level of nihilism doesn't resonate with someone who sells an afterlife.

"Catching up on some yard work?" His wandering gaze does find my dirt-caked hands, however.

"Eh, yeah. Helps my mind process the events, I guess. It's only been two days—no, three."

"Oh. Ooooh. Right. Well, I'm here if there's anything you'd like to, what is the word, express."

"Thank you, Father, and I'll hold you to that, but it is getting late."

"Yes, I suppose it is. Would it be an affront to your lamentation if I were to visit you in the coming days? At a more reasonable hour?" He politely hands me back the washcloth with a nod so gentle that I question if it is even voluntary.

"Just knock, if you don't mind."

"Certainly, sir. Certainly."

He fiddles with his hat before he puts it on his head and turns his back to me.

ROOTS RUN DEEP

"And please, take care of more than just your yard."

"I'll try, Father," and he's gone. Back into the mist. His shape vanishes instantly in the night.

The rain will keep the creature hydrated, and that little lapse in activity has killed my momentum. I feel like I can fall asleep on my feet. Maybe it is time. I'm not sleeping in the bedroom or the living room, so I guess that leaves the dining room. That's fine. There's a big enough chair in the corner, and I'll grab a blanket from the laundry room on my way over.

I pause on the garage steps.

There's no one else waiting for me at the garage, is there?

No.

Good.

I massage the wall-mounted button until it registers my touch.

The garage door lowers and seals me into my home.

Huh.

I can't remember the last time I looked at the garage as a needed space. It's merely been a corridor to walk through for so long. We had even given up parking the car inside. I do feel better. Not good, but a dash elated. Even talking through it with that zombie of a priest felt cathartic. I might finish that chiminea someday.

I wish I had been thinking about something else before I stepped into the laundry room. I would have been more prepared if I remained sullen. Now, I'm emotionally blindsided by the sight. Frozen in awe at what used to be our laundry room.

It's been commandeered by life.

Pearl white flowers with black stems and indigo buds invade every corner and reach for every surface. The house sprouted veins while I was looking away and I'm standing in its heart. I would enjoy the harmonious melding of nature and tile, but I live in this Norman Rockwell nightmare.

J. KRAWCZYK

Most frightening of all is my own reflection.
It's not alone.
Between me and the mirror stands a frail nervous system of black vines, echoing my frame and reaching for a coat with petal fingers.

THE DINING ROOM

I TRIED TO SLEEP. Emphasis on 'tried' and an emphasis on 'emphasis.' There was no real attempt. I knew I was just acting out what I should be doing rather than doing the act. It was a pathetic ballet; alternating between staring at the ceiling and staring at the wall. And, as comfy as this armchair is, there's no amount of reclining that will make it a bed.

I'm just afraid to look at anything else with everything that's happened. It's too much to compute. My mind can't catalog it all and so it desperately replays images and interactions, trying to make sense. My body has nothing left. It's just being pulled around by my brain's neurosis. A marionette tied to a puppy.

I did fill out the form for the backhoe, though. According to the sunlight creeping its way across the ceiling, it should be here in a few hours.

It's back there, far away behind the eyes: a pit where I store my body's appeals for rest. It's compounding. Pulsating. The pleas will soon swell into demands, and after that, we embark on a new horizon. That's where it will become dangerous. Well, more dangerous. A broken threshold that no amount of rest will mend. Permanent damage. Maybe coffee will be an appropriate arbitration. At least it'll give me something to do.

My joints don't ache, but they are stiff. They're numbed by the cold sensation emanating from my gut. Movement briefly thaws them, so I have to keep the momentum rolling, or I'll freeze into a sleepy mannequin.

My order of operations is off. I filter hot water through a French press. Coffee requires coffee. The button to grind the beans is almost too labor-intensive. All of my focus goes into holding down the rubber button. The throbbing mechanical pulverization is excruciating in every sense. It hurts to see, let alone hear. Even the vibrations of holding down the button sting my digits. I can't take it anymore. I stop the grind way too early and dump the scant coffee into the hot water. This time, I'll wait. I need a respite from sensation.

But then I find something that does the opposite. That flower from yesterday. There are dozens behind our kitchen appliances. They're sprouting from every corner of our kitchen, shattering their life through the grout and tile.

I open the kitchen cabinets. Each of them has the same result. Somehow, without sunlight, each pantry contains dishes entangled in blooming charcoal vines with ivory leaves. The living room is on the other side of this wall. What could that possibly look like? If the creature's branches have thrived within the tight quarters of our laundry room, what could it do with more space and large windows? They feel the same as the creature's skin. Organic but closer to petrified wood than living flesh. And the flowers share more than just the color of ivory. They can bend with enough pressure, but it's like trying to manipulate the rubber of a tire.

How can this support life? How can this be life?

I'm too tired to find an excuse not to check the living room. But am I ready? It's where this all started, but it is getting out of control. I need to know what I'm dealing with.

You're dealing with the death of your soul mate. That's it. That's everything. There's nothing that can take priority over that. Not even a creature beyond science invading your home. Still, I'm rounding the corner to the living room.

The first thing I see are vines against the fireplace brick. I keep moving, but I don't want to see anymore. It's like knowing of an injury before seeing it. I wince in anticipation, but I also crane my neck around the corner. I won't feel the pain until I see the damage, so why am I about to look?

"Mr. Carver?"

If my senses weren't attuned to a potential flight or fight, I might not have been able to hear Mia's thin voice from behind the door.

"Oh my, be right there!" I redirect all my fears of the unknown into the anxiety of being known. "Please, I'm coming! Hold on!"

I initiate a sprint but immediately realize I put forty yards of energy into a four-yard hallway. That same amount of energy is necessary not to bulldoze Mia. Better the floor than the grandfather clock, I suppose. I go down hard and loud.

"Hey, hey, hey, hey, what happened? You okay?" Mia disclaims as she enters our house of her own accord. She kneels down to my aid.

"Yes, yes, sorry. Sorry. I'm fine. I'm fine," I lie and I find my way back up to my feet. Mia offers a forearm for support, but I pretend to miss it. There's a very specific pain that comes from hardwood. Your body rarely ever makes violent contact with something so flat and smooth. It's almost more humiliating than agonizing. But, ow. Left knee, left elbow, right wrist. Where the bones are closest to the skin, a sparkle of pins and needles dance over a swelling heat in the cockles of my joints. My body does a bad job at lying.

"Why don't you take a seat for a minute?"

"No, no, it's okay. Moving helps alleviate some of the aches. Coffee? I was brewing coffee."

"I mean, firstly, hello," Mia gestures with the manilla envelope she has tucked under her arm.

"Hello," I respond through my teeth.

"And second, sure. As long as you keep it light. Is that it over there? I can grab it."

"If you don't mind—" impossible flowers spawned by an unfathomable beast are in the kitchen. "Ah, you know what, I got it. It'll help me shake off the sting," which is not untrue, but, by god, I'd rather be sitting. "Please, take a seat."

"So, have you managed to rest since we've spoken?"

"I managed to not move for a few hours, if that counts."

"Baby steps."

"Suppose."

The mugs from yesterday are in the sink, so they're about to experience deja vu after a quick rinse.

"So, I have some release forms from the hospital and an acquisition form for the funeral home closest to you," Mia says as she sinks into her chair and my bed.

"Thank you." I hand her the mug, and she hands me the envelope. I can feel that there's already a pen inside. I bet they do that to make it easy for the widow. The last thing I want to worry about is if a pen works. I don't honestly know the last time I used my hands for pen and paper. I used to write my name multiple times a day. Now, I almost don't know what my signature looks like.

I sit at the dining room table, not only to look over her documents, but also to divert her eyes away from the hallway. I'm not sure how fast those vines grow, but if they branch out past the living room, I'll have some explaining to do.

"There's also an application for a death certificate you'll need to fill out."

"This one here?"

I know it is.

I just want to feel normal.

"Yes, sir. That's it." Mia says, raising her voice for 'it.' This process makes me feel like I'm signing up for a gym.

"Will do."

Death Certificate.

Not even.

An application for a Death Certificate.

Dying isn't enough to be considered dead. Not a diploma or an award, but a certificate. An acknowledgment that you no longer exist. Your corpse isn't even yours. I guess that says something about the soul, but it just feels so dystopian. Alex is no longer the person who shared their life with Edward. They're not the other half of an impregnable routine. Edward's entire persona was built upon being Alex's life partner, but Edward is now just a lone residual. Incomplete. One card of the two-person house of cards. How is Edward supposed to stay upright? How is Edward supposed to balance himself back up on his own? And, at this point, Why?

Maybe she is just a certificate now. The amount of processed shit we eat? I have no idea what's actually in my food or how it's made. And why would we? We've been evolving for seven million years. Seven million years of meat, plants, and water, then BAM! I don't know how a Wendy's Frosty came to be, but I could eat one every day. Our bodies didn't develop to eat shit and breath smoke. I'm surprised we're not all just dropping dead from forces outside of our control, but somehow our responsibility. Maybe we're all just victims in a bureaucratic ant farm of fear, and death is our retirement.

Yeah, I'm eating poison, but who the hell wants to farm?

Modern living. Bathing in the consequences of a new, old normal. They're picketing the same shit Alex and I did forty years ago. We hit a comfortable equilibrium, and we're just going to keep spinning those wheels until they melt. And here I am: a crossover from a bygone era. The last survivor of birth, life, death, and the first old man in birth, life, Armageddon. An everyday cog in the *eh, fuck it, we kind of tried* doomsday clock.

Huh, that's what my signature looks like.

"How many do you want?" Mia asks.

"Pardon me?"

"Death Certificates. You need more than one."

"Oh um . . . three?"

"Five's probably safer."

"Oh, um, funeral home, the hospital . . . ?"

"Your lawyer, your accountant, social security?"

"We don't need those."

"Um, I'm pretty sure you do, even if there's nothing to inherit."

"Five it is." Cog in a wheel.

"Whoa-ho? What's going on here?"

I almost stand up when hearing Mia's question.

"What's what?" I brace, not sure how to tackle the onslaught of questions about to come my way. I should have told her to come back tomorrow.

"Oh, sorry. The coffee. It's light."

Oh my. My pretentious cerebral tangent almost had me forget I'm an idiot.

"Oh, yes. Sorry."

"You're a man of your word," Mia says as she sips her coffee of hot off-color water.

"I've been abiding by the caffeine decoction a little too amorously lately." Those words just fell out of me. Some part of me is trying to compensate for my sluggishness.

"Well, you have every right to do what you have to. It's a crisis scenario."

"Don't know if it's a crisis. One of us was eventually going to go first."

"For sure, it's a crisis."

"No. It's a fact of life."

"Dying is, surviving is the crisis."

I open my mouth, but no retort follows. The slurry of halfhearted responses just slosh around inside my skull. A spinning dryer of tattered left socks. With no momentum or expansion beyond the knee-jerk, the flimsy thoughts shrivel and die. I wouldn't be surprised if I remained frozen in place for an uncomfortable moment. Uncomfortable for Mia. I'm too preoccupied with being a pillar of indecision.

I am in a crisis, after all.

"Do you think I can get a splash more?"

"Hm, yeah, sure."

She stands up to get it herself, and I panic. There's no tactful way to stop her from going into the kitchen. She's already on her feet and closer to the press.

"Thanks, I'm just enjoying the warmth in my hands, you know?"

"I let it go cold more often than not because of that—"

Shit, she's in the kitchen.

"—sometimes, I make a whole new pot, you know, but at the same time, it feels like a waste of coffee—"

She's pouring with eyes still on me.

"—but I like a smokey bean rather than a floral one, and that's usually cheaper, so it doesn't bother me too much. That smokier flavor comes from a Ugandan bean, so that's why most gas station coffee has a similar aroma because it's such a cheaper bean—"

Please sit back down.

"—not that I don't like a more flavourful bean, the Ethiopian bean has a blueberry quality, which is quite nice, but that's a little pricey, so I make do. And I always wanted to try how they roast beans in a pan, but you know, I wouldn't know where to start, but then again, I suppose you can use a regular frying pan—"

She's coming back, but it's still risky.

"—Ethiopia, weird, right? You would assume with their climate that their bean would be smokier, but no, blueberries. Not that I know that much of Ethiopia's landscape outside of TV. I wonder if it's similar to scotch."

Oh, thank god. She's back in her chair. Had to cash in my Rambling-Old-Man card to achieve that distraction.

"What about scotch?" she asks.

Oh, god, she was actually listening. "Oh, um, scotch flavor profiles differ from region to region, and I suppose it'd be similar to coffee. Climate and altitude and vegetation and whatnot."

" . . . but in Scotland?"

"Oh, yes. I don't know what goes on with Ethiopian Scotch."

"Hm," Mia coos as she nestles her cup of warmth. We both detach from our back and forth, and I complete the forms.

Numbers. That's all I'm filling out. Social Security, dates, addresses. Eons from now, when aliens study our way of life, they'll assume we worshiped forms. Just endless paperwork to receive more paperwork so we can exist another day to earn a new form. Life isn't measured by your last breath, but by your last form, so you can transcend into your own form. A pamphlet cataloging where and when we were. Death is truly your final form. It's anything but enlightening to know that I, one day, will be a row of numbers in a series of boxes. I just haven't a clue who will be filling out mine.

"Alrighty, I think I'm done."

"Okay. Thank you." As Mia stands, something catches her eye from the front window. "It looks like you have something being dropped off?"

I turn to see an effervescent orange trailer backing into our driveway by an equally garish, lime green pickup truck. That color scheme, coupled with the blinking red tail lights, is an affront to sight.

"Wow, they're punctual."

"Thank god I parked on the street."

"Do you want to take the mug with you?" I ask, motioning to Mia's coffee with her manilla envelope of paperwork.

"No need." She trades me an empty mug for the envelope. "Thank you, though. It hit the spot."

"Anytime."

"I'll drop these off tomorrow, and the funeral home will give you a ring with the remaining information."

"Okay, thank you, Mia."

"Alright . . . " Mia extends her hand. "Until I need more light coffee."

"My doors always open, apparently." I shake her hand before I open the door for her. No wonder she likes a hot mug. Her hands are frigid and clammy. Strong though. I guess grip strength is a necessity in a hospital.

"Please take care, Edward." She steps off my stoop and walks toward the car. She has to walk around the nauseating truck and trailer combo.

The wiry driver, wearing a denim jacket over his safety coveralls, steps out of the pickup. His work attire appropriately clashes with the rest of his equipment. Sky blue with reflective neon stripes. He gives me a wave.

"I'll be right with you," I yelp as I close the door behind me. Funny. My enthusiasm for this project is almost non-existent, even if it is an unprecedented anomaly. Similar to that sobering drop-off of ambition the next morning. Projects are so much more tantalizing at night. That boundless potential is so alluring when you don't have to exert effort.

My wallet is in my jacket, and my jacket's in the laundry, and our laundry room is currently a jungle.

Oh my.

The nervous system of vines and flowers has moved. It's now reaching for the backdoor's handle. It gives me room to get to my jacket, at least. I catch a glimpse of the living room from the laundry room closet. Vines. Maybe it'll be different enough that I can dissociate.

Oh my. Oh my, oh my, oh my.

That figure of vegetative sinew. That's me. Or, *was* me. The creature is mimicking what I've been doing, but not just since I discovered it. There are two more entangled plant figures nestled in embrace on our couch.

My head on Alex's lap.

That's what it is.

I'm looking at a sinewy recreation of us.

That was our spot.

That's us.

THE SHED

I'M STANDING IN a pit about seven feet in the earth with an overcast fourteen-foot circumference above me. Not bad, considering I was abandoning this project three hours ago.

I've finally found the bottom of this beast.

Well, I've found the bottom of a part of the beast. It, itself, might be a mile-long monstrosity. The appendage I've excavated is about twice my width, and it looks like it grows thicker the deeper it goes into the soil. It now has enough room to maneuver and coil three hundred and sixty degrees, which is just as gratifying as it is terrifying. It does gently watch me dig it out of its confines, and it assists me in getting in and out of this hole, but it's also a creature I don't fully understand, with independent thought I certainly don't understand.

Cows are nurtured by farmers only to be slaughtered.

Recreating past memories to incentivize my help has crossed my mind. Like a free sample from a drug dealer. But what's the endgame for this creature? Will it eventually get up and walk away?

I doubt it, but at the same, it doesn't matter.

I sat in the living room for an hour before moving the excavator back here. I soaked myself in our past. Alex and I laid on that couch for hours before bed. Sometimes we just stayed there through the night. Sleeping in each other's arms. TV, reading, listening to records, talking. That position was ours and ours alone. Heaven encapsulated. If this thing keeps providing me glimpses of our life, it can eat me for all I care. It's worth whatever it has in store for me.

However, another root, one that isn't a primordial, subterranean colossus, is obstructing my progress. It's from the white spruce where our garden meets the forest. It's a gorgeous tree but it has become untempered over the years. Its languid pine has enveloped most of our shed and its fallen cones have painted our green sod brown. Cosmetically appealing, but logistically invasive. Other plants have suffered from its dominion, and I won't let it happen to our guest.

"Looks like some jerk's got you tangled."

I make eye contact with the 'face' of the beast. It's not quite a face; being pockmarked by eye-like divots and sinewy mouths that repeat throughout its body. A living statue of sidewinding complexity.

"I think there's a jab saw in the shed," I tell the face and it coils in the shed's direction. Fashions a jagged ramp out of its branches. In the last few days, I've talked to this thing more than any person I've seen. I don't know if I'm just projecting emotions onto it, but it seems to grasp what I'm saying. It's going to have to help me if I need to get the backhoe in the pit.

I can feel its system of roots shift beneath my feet. As gentle as the motion is, a quick pang of nausea hits my gut. I'm seasick on land. I have to be the only human on earth who's not in awe at the sight; roots shifting on their own to form a crude step ladder. Being mystified serves no purpose.

"Thank you," I say as I grip its branches for balance.

I dust myself off as I step out of the pit. I'm more dirt than man, so this is just a sanitary reflex. When I look down into the pit, the branches relax back into their original position. It's comforting to know it takes effort to help me. I'm not servicing some apathetic deity, but something that requires energy conservation. That gives me a little hope.

"Gimme a sec."

It's been so long since I've opened the shed's door that it's warped into the frame. Untreated wood pulverized by decades of rain, snow, and heat will do that. The offset has wedged the top right corner into the doorway, and even if it wasn't obstructed, two neglected tumors of rust have replaced the hinges.

"Awe, shit. This is-oh my." The wood doesn't budge as I slam my heft near the doorknob. I'll break before the door does.

Nausea returns to my gut while I ponder toward the shed. My feet. The ground moves from under me once again, and the shed creeks from its shifting foundation.

"What're you, what're you, what're you—" I struggle to stay upright as more pine rains down from the spruce.

"Okay, not for me. Sitting down." Shortly after my rear end hits the dirt, the door shimmies in a way that liberates it from its frame.

I turn to see my friend peeking at me from its hole.

"Well, look at you."

I'm slow to my feet.

"Got me dirty again, but, you know—"

I grip onto the doorknob and yank.

"I appreciate the hand."

The rust chips off the hinges, and the door clumsily opens toward me.

"Or tendril."

I stand in a darkened entrance to a dust-kissed memory.

Just like our home, the creature's vines and flowers have invited themselves into our shed. Stark rays of sunlight shine through the cracks, illuminating gentle gillings, dancing in the air. One of the first things I see is a handsaw, but my attention fixates on the six-foot figure assembled of black stems and shed debris. With a garden rake for one hand, the handsaw for the other, and a rubber mallet for a head, my doppelgänger stands frozen in place, hunched over an abandoned project.

"You're getting better." I walk over to my porous reflection. "Clever with the hand rake for a hand."

Oh my.

I don't know if it's because the creature's closer to the shed than the living room, but I can see the figure move. It's slight, like watching goosebumps form on the skin, but it very much is moving. At the speed of a glacier, the vines coil and bend.

A zucchini fence. That's what I was working on. We wanted to try to grow them vertically, and I thought it'd be nice to have a chiminea during the cooler days. We could also burn some of the rubbish left over from my process.

Process? Listen to me. Somewhere in there, that art degree refuses to die.

I'm afraid one abandoned project has led to another, and now I'm standing in its half-assed wake. What stopped me? Was sitting in self-pity better than working in self-pity? At least, I could have been disappointed in something rather than being disappointing.

I reach for the handsaw in the vine man's hand.

"Shit!" I yelp as the tool pulls away. "Come on!"

It's still slow, so I'm able to get a grip on the wooden handle of the jab saw.

"It's okay. I need this to help you."

It's an impressive grip. I try to wrench the tool-free, but I just embolden the vines to tighten.

"Okay, okay, okay, why don't you—"

I yank, and my hand slips to the serrated teeth.

"Oh, shit! Jesus Christ! Shit!"

I don't think I've hit the bone, but I was close. I don't want to look at it. As soon as I do, the pain is real. So I want to.

The tendril releases its grasp on the saw and reaches for my injured hand.

"No, no, no. You've done enough, thank you."

I simultaneously reel my bloodied fist back and grab the saw with my intact fingers.

"Thank you!" I disclaim as I tuck the saw under my armpit. Finding an old washcloth in the bundle of vines and flowers, I keep my eyes on the figure as I mend my wound. One, because I want to avoid another altercation, and two, I don't even want to acknowledge the severity of my injury. There's a task at hand, and it takes priority over mine.

As I move back toward the pit, its gaze seems to follow my lacerated hand.

"It's fine. I'm fine." My peripherals catch the abrupt transformation from pale blue to dark red in the cloth. This could be bad. And it's not like the jab saw is free of rust. Tetanus will have to wait. The creature's attention stays on my hand, so it doesn't provide me with a makeshift stairwell to descend into the pit.

"Fine, whatever, I got it," I say to myself as I slide myself in the hole, like a toddler scooting their way down the stairs. Slathered in mud, I march to the obtrusive root. Simple enough. I'll saw it down the middle and shear it away from my friend here.

"Ready?"

Why should I even ask?

Some of my blood remains on the blade as it mangles its way through the bark. Dormant grief erupts from the repetition. I inadvertently cross that line that separates composure and rage. Everything that's happened. Everything that's happening. All those potential avenues of life vanish with each stroke of the blade, leaving only dwindling roads to nowhere. There's so little left for me except for the grief. That's boundless. There's no bottom to my well of regret and frustration. One eating the other. Over and over, in a constant compounding ouroboros of despair. I lose myself and, therefore, time. I didn't exist for a moment, and it cost me. I've cut through the root and into my friend.

"Oh, no, no, no, no, no, no, I'm sorry. I'm so sorry."

It doesn't move as I touch its wound. The laceration gives me a glimpse of what's inside of its husk.

"Are you okay? Are you—" I grip the root of the spruce and pry it away for my friend's body.

"Oh no, you're bleeding. You're bleeding. I didn't mean to—"

It's not. I am, and it's glistening atop the monster's gash.

"Oh my, I'm sorry. Are you okay? Show me you're okay." I wipe away my blood from the wound as it splays open. It's the same as its mouth. A slate-like exterior with a fleshy and fibrous interior. But wait. Something new. Veins. It has veins. Shimmering, metallic veins. Gold? It has literal golden veins. How is this possible? Out of curiosity, I touch the flesh beneath its skin. It's dense yet malleable, reminiscent of dough before it's kneaded. It doesn't show me any signs of pain, so I continue to examine its makeshift muscles. It's beautiful in its complexity. A bird's eye view of golden rivers in a blood-red forest.

What are you?

Alive.

That's what it is as it jostles and writhes its enormous protoplasmic chassis. I skitter back as the earth moves from under me. Not just under me, but everywhere. This might be it. The unceremonious end I've been crawling toward.

I can hear its size and it's immense. It slithers its way to freedom and unfurls toward the clouds like a cobra made of timber. The offshoots of roots stay planted in the ground as it billows in its newfound expanse.

Oh my. It's taller than our house. More eyes and mouths emerge from the ground.

I panic. People aren't supposed to see this.

I use the suspended vines to climb out of the pit and roll onto level ground. Please, don't seize. No back pain. Override whatever injury I sustain.

"Hey, no! Stop!"

Our shed is toppling over from the creature's motions.

The snapping bark of adjacent trees echoes throughout the surrounding forest.

"Please, stop!"

A crack louder than thunder rings in my ears before the spruce lurches away from the ground and collapses behind the shed. Its root system tears the shed apart from the inside. A titanic shift hoists the structure a few feet into the air and crashes it down into a heap of flimsy debris.

"No! NO! How dare you!" I holler as I get to my feet. "How dare—"

But it's for naught.

The forest behind the shed shares a similar fate. Trees topple, and branches snap. Treetops sway under the beast's influence as far as my eyes can see. I'm watching a city of life desperately fight to survive.

"Oh my . . . I can't . . . I can't!"

The stoic misanthrope wilts away, revealing the lonely and scared widow underneath. I run back into the laundry room and slam the door behind me.

"Stop! Please stop!"

The house shudders, and I kneel to the ground.

"Please!"

I beg. I place a hand on the tile floor.

"Please! Stop!"

And then it does.

My heartbeat is now the loudest thing in the room. It may not be audible to someone else's ears, but it's all I can hear.

Focus. Remember how to breathe before you stand up.

Shutting my eyes, I let the darkness slow my spinning vision, let my stomach decide what to do with that weak coffee. Thank god I didn't eat.

I open my eyes and my blurry hand is the first thing I see. Lights are too bright, shadows are a void, and clarity misses its target. I know there are nails on my fingers. I just need to find them.

There.

Detail.

Flickers of clouded light flutter between my eyes and my hand until acuity prevails. With my bearings under me, I lift my hand off the ground. I'm not ready to stand yet; my breath is on par with my heartbeat. The sight of my bloody handprint on the tile gives me pause.

There we go.

Focus on that.

Breathe.

Fill your lungs and hold that air in your chest.

Exhale.

Do it again.

And again.

Okay. Stand up.

I had been avoiding looking at my wound to free my friend. Now, I'm going to mend my wound to distract myself from the Lovecraftian nightmare I've unleashed.

Oh my, in the three hours I was outback, the animal-flesh-vegetation has taken over more of the house. No more coffee visits for Mia. Our hallways look like we're experimenting with an indoor wine vineyard. There's still plenty of room to get around, however. Not sure if that's intentional or the nature of its development. What I do know for sure is in a day or two, our home will be little more than our garden.

Our downstairs bathroom is clear, however. I suspect it's too compact and too far away from the backyard for the beast to reach. I always hated the fluorescent lighting against the white tile. It is too bright and makes it feel like I'm brushing my teeth in an institution. I'm still too afraid to go upstairs. You have to walk through the bedroom to do that, and that's a bridge too far for my current psyche to cross. The harsh, unforgiving light tightens the vice against my sleep-deprived skull. I'll just grab our makeshift medical kit from under the sink and mend myself in the kitchen.

Let's see what a thirty-year-old ointment and gauze can

do. The smell under the sink matches the look of our bathroom. Sterile and stale. Just unpleasant in every sense. For containers, Alex and I would cut milk cartons in half and use them to store supplies. Weren't we hip and environmentally conscious, thinks the man who freed a beast of the apocalypse.

Here we are. Gauze, bandaids, topical antibacterial, and a small stack of folded papers.

What are these? Age made them frail to the touch and muted brown. *Alex* is written in cursive. I do not recognize the writing. I open it with little to no caution and the first thing I read under a lofty, handwritten soliloquy is *XOXO, Derek.*

THE BATHROOM

IT MAKES SENSE NOW.

I should have trusted my intuition. The distance. The isolation. It wasn't a delusion. Alex's focus was divided, and I became a roommate rather than a mate. All those years of unjust shame, I'm not the one who capitulated. I'm not the one that betrayed you. I thought I did. Somewhere within, I thought I had given up, but now I know. The hollowness one feels when one confronts the truth. When your foundation becomes quicksand, you just become inert. Information should be able to erase your being.

Unfortunately, here I am.

Sitting on the bathroom floor and staring at my undoing.

There are three letters, and judging by the brittleness of the paper, they were written around the same time. Once white and malleable, unfolding them now risks shattering the dry paper. They're romantic. That makes them worse. If they were merely perverse, I could chalk them up to erotic compulsions. I was always hesitant to be more promiscuous in the bedroom. Even thinking about it made me blush. Now, my heart pumps ice when I imagine Alex begging for Derek to have his way with her.

There's continual use of words like *soul, heart* and *love*. At first, I dread reading them, but my many insecurities collide at an impasse. It's so strange that unyielding rage can be snuffed out by the end of a sentence. Only my empty shell remains. I have yet to mend my injured hand, yet I feel no sting. It's there, but it's so remote it's not even an inconvenience. I didn't know what to do with myself after she died, and now I'm completely lost. Is there any more? Was Derek the one and only? Did I steal her from her soulmate? What else don't I know?

I plunge my hands back under the sink. The corroded rust causes me no mind as I yank every toiletry onto the tile floor. My open wound was already threatened by tetanus and infection. Why stop now?

Nothing.

Well, what about the linen closet? I tell myself I'm in a state of controlled anger, but when I thrust open the closet, the doorknob punches a hole in the wall. Towels and sheets folded over a decade ago produce a stale odor, reminiscent of an abandoned office building.

What would I know of an office? I was too cowardly to pursue my artistic passions, so why would I ever step foot in an office? Endless driving for me, thank you. Years of my life dedicated to highway lines and headlights. I didn't even have to interact with anyone. All I had to do was reliably deliver prepackaged bread. I just needed to ensure nothing changed for the worse or the better.

Sure, honey, have an affair! Just as long as dinner is on the table!

But not even a table.

A couch.

In front of the TV.

Let me just drive fourteen hours a day while you fucked our lifelong friend, so I can silently sit in front of an idiot box and shovel carbs into my useless face. No need to thank me for abandoning the one thing that gave me a pulse. As long as I deliver our bank account bread by delivering bread, do whatever you'd like!

It's all worth it for that vague disappointment in your eyes.

Good for you, Edward. You did it.

I'm not sure how much time has passed, but most of

our bathroom is on the floor. Ravaged by blind frustration, cabinet doors have been torn from their hinges, toiletries jettisoned from their shelves, and mirrors shattered against the blood-slick tile and crumbled love letters. I'm out of breath. Despite the reprieve into lucidity, my mind oscillates between self-destruction and external rage. At least I didn't find another note.

Where else should I look?

Our bedroom.

Is it time?

Am I angry enough?

Our?

Our bedroom?

It's never been *ours* at all, has it?

It's always been mine.

My bedroom.

And it's meaningless now. It's merely a monument to a wasted life. This whole place is. This isn't a home, and it never has been.

"HEY!" I bark. "You can hear me!"

I march out of the bathroom and head for the backdoor. I trample whatever vines stand in my way. The laundry room has become a jungle, so it's a struggle to continue onward.

"Let me through! I need to-I need to-I need to—!"

Life recoils as I thrash. The meek roots retreat in the wake of my sorrow. It's the first clear night in some time. The stars blaze so bright I almost lose sight of my mission.

"Take it down! All of it! It's not anyone's! Take it down! Destroy it!" I wail to the beast.

Its unfurled body towers over me, looking down on me from the sky. I've been looking down on it since I found it. Now, I'm looking up. Its skin is so pitch-dark that it's a shadow upon even the looming night. A silhouette within a void.

"Take the—our—my—the house—TAKE THE HOUSE DOWN! Destroy it! Come on! Turn it to rubble. Keep growing. Take it over! It's not anyone's anymore! Never has been! That's what you're doing, right? Taking over! Well, good for you! It's yours! Always has been! I don't need it!"

It merely watches me. Quietly. Gently. Can't have that.

I grab the abandoned hand saw at the edge of the creature's pit and hurl it at one of its many faces. It quivers at the act, but it's more emotional than physical.

"I don't need your pity! Come on! Ruin it! Ruin it all! It's got nothing left to offer!"

My arms flail in my house's direction, but the monster keeps its attention on me.

"What?! No?! I'll start for ya!?"

Gripping the shovel that started it all, I drive it through the window to the laundry room. It only takes one plunge for the glass to shatter, reminding me of my injury. Paltry in a contest with my neglected internal wounds. They're deep and rotten; poisoning my mind with comfort.

This house was a mistake.

"It all led to this? All of it? For this? Fuck it! Bring it all down!"

Seeing my pathetic attempts to damage a whole house with a shovel, I chuck it away. Think bigger. I have a primordial colossus of the apocalypse at my disposal. Use it.

"Come on, now! Get In on this!"

I fill my hands with two of its many offshoot branches and heave.

"Come on! Please, take it! Take it away! Please! I'm begging you!"

I writhe and jerk and pull, digging my heels deeper into the ground. My body forgoes self-preservation, and I can feel a few teeth crack under my strain. It doesn't budge, but my sciatic nerve eventually does.

Pain returns to reassure my mind that it still has a body.

"Agh! No! Please!"

A knee is forced to the ground.

ROOTS RUN DEEP

"No, no, no, no—" I attempt to stand, but that just fuels my body's rebellion. My kneecap lifts about an inch off the ground before my shoulder and temple takes its place. It's been a while since I've felt this ringing between my ears. This may be a concussion.

So, that checks off everything. Every part of my body, inside and out, is on fire. Throbbing, stabbing, aching, burning. All of it. Every form of agony my useless body and misguided mind can register invades my person, and all I can think about is Alex.

I miss you so much. I'm sorry. I'm so sorry. You deserved more than me.

My nails scrape across the dirt.

I can't move, so why am I moving? Already clutching onto a fist of soil, I release it to grab another in hopes of gaining my bearings. Nothing. I'm moving against my will. The pain in my lower back restrains my entire nervous system. I can't crane my neck. The muscles surrounding my throat cease and shudder in the attempt.

You never realize how your entire body is interconnected until something's wrong. Your body communicates with itself, and right now, it's a unified effort to stop me, no matter the cost. Thirty-six trillion cells and seven trillion nerves unanimously agree that I am its biggest threat. Me. The most significant danger to me is myself. That sentiment remains even as I see the ground rise above me.

"Pulleese, naaa, stawwwp—" My jaw follows my neck as if in sparks of acidic pain.

It's dragging me into the pit. I'm numb from pain but can feel the pressure as thin, steely tendrils tighten around my ankles and thighs. I can't revolt in any way. I can't even ask it to stop. I'm at the mercy of its enigmatic spirit. It's under my clothes. The only reason I know that is because the sleeve in my peripherals billows from the movement underneath. Movement I can't possibly achieve.

I vanish for an instant. The hard and unceremonious

thud at the bottom of the pit short circuits my nervous system. There's a limit to sensation, and I have crossed it. I wish I could be on my back. I want to see the sky in my final moments, at least. The sight of my hand immediately cancels that wish.

I don't want to see anything anymore.

My friend. Its vines. They're under my skin.

The sight gives me the strength to turn over. My joints wrench with the aid of foreign antigens. My body is no longer just my body. Boring incisions in my flesh, it explores the frontier between skin and muscle. A vast new enterprise of tissue.

It's yours.

Take it.

I have nothing left to offer.

Breath leaves my body and doesn't return.

Just out of reach of my focus, the last sight to touch my eyes is the stars. Softly shimmering in a hazy universe.

This is it.

I missed the exact moment, but my soul has surrendered. Every instinct rests, and the great mystery is invited into Edward Carver.

The last bit of acuity I can maintain is fractured shapes of starlight dissolving into a phylum of anemic color, eventually fading into darkness. I don't have the strength to close my eyes, but it doesn't matter. The world graciously withers away for me. I thought I knew black, but this is black.

It's consuming. Intoxicating. Warm. Words lose meaning. Thoughts flutter violently before succumbing. Awareness liquidates.

Iamnothing.

Neverwasnoreveragain.

Nothing.

THE BEDROOM

Oh MY, this is humiliating.

I'm not dreaming.

I'm not dead.

I'm not confused.

I'm in bed.

There's a tsunami of questions to follow, but coming to terms with death only to wake up alive takes precedence. Accepting life is more of a challenge, comparatively speaking. Dying was, at least, a release. Now, I have to reclaim responsibilities. Even the simplest of actions feels too big. Who knew something like breathing could burden someone? Disappointing in hindsight.

I remain in bed for as long as I can. I didn't wake up under the covers, so I nestle myself under the duvet and wool throw rug. The cool blankets melt against my skin as if it were the first time. It's so nice. It is so gentle and smooth that it redefines the concepts. I feel like a child. Unencumbered by thought; I've expressed it all in the last seventy-two hours. There is nothing left to repress. I just want to stay here. Hold in this moment and relish in the emptiness.

I wish I could've gotten here on my own, but I needed the assistance of loss, betrayal, and a life form unrestrained by modern science. It's not until I have to visit the bathroom that I consider getting out of bed. Even when the pressure hits my bladder, I remain steadfast until it's on the verge of unbearable. I sit up, and there's not a single shred of discomfort. It doesn't seem possible. Maybe I am dead. It would help explain what's happening in our bedroom.

Hm.

Our.

I thought the placid glow was from daybreak, but all the windows display a night sky. It's either early night or late morning because the sun has yet to even consider rising. Otherworldly foliage makes up most of our bedroom, so it's hard to find a lamp. White flowers with green berries on black vines. Everywhere. There's not a free inch of wall space that isn't visited by life. Its beauty has escaped me until this moment. I'm not quite sure how long I was asleep, but I'm refreshed enough to know it was substantial.

Prioritize sleep, Edward. Please. It even simplifies grief.

Oh my . . .

The light is not emitting from lamps, but from bulbs. Literal, organic orbs, pregnant with light, are intermittently glowing amongst swollen branches.

I get to my feet to inspect the phenomenon, but something else snags my attention. My joints have been replaced with oil and iron. I don't even feel them. They're just there. I just feel whole. I'm just one piece. I'm half-compelled to test my mobility, but the light prods at my curiosity again.

It's such a gentle light. A miniature sun that massages your eyes and swaddles your soul. There's liquid behind a translucent ball of marble. I tap the miracle of nature. It's hot to the touch. Scolding, if held for more than a moment.

Something just as surprising as the light source is my own hand.

"Oh, um, uh. Wow."

Where once was a gash that required stitches now resides a charcoal sliver of sutures. It's more than a bandage; the creature has mended my wound, though its material is embedded within my hand, and the tiniest glints of gold outline the otherworldly stitches. Grazing over it with my fingertips, I can barely feel the edge of where the creature begins and I end. Sensation remains. The monstrous skin graft feels the finger stroke, just as my flesh does around it.

Hm, it's replaced the crease that was my lifeline. Somewhere behind a lifetime of bashfulness, I've always wanted a tattoo. Finding a design that seemed significant to me and me alone seemed impossible. Lucky me. What can be more significant than this?

On my way to the bathroom, I grab a discarded pair of pajama pants. They're red fleece speckled with holly for the Christmas season. A present from Alex that somehow stayed in rotation for the last decade. Was it the luck of the draw, or do I just not acknowledge that I like the feel? There's a cool embrace similar to the blanket's . . .

What's happening? Why am I waxing poetic over blankets and pajamas? This can't just be the result of a good night's sleep. Maybe my friend out back supplied me with a psychedelic? If it were able to mend my wound as well as hoist me into my bedroom, why not also produce psychoactive substances?

I don't feel high. Maybe it's just the elation of releasing turmoil, emotional and physical. I'm sad, for sure, but tapped out of resentment. When was the last time I truly unpacked any emotional baggage? It's all been reactive and not reflective. When was the last time I cried? Maybe I'm not feeling empty, but weightless.

"Oh no. Oh, god. This is . . . oh god."

I take it back. I take it all back.

This could be bad.

No wonder I feel so different. I am different.

"It just keeps going. Holy shit."

I'm terrified to discover that the sliver of root is not confined to my hand.

The bathroom mirror isn't big enough to capture the

whole pattern. My entire back is ingrained in wiry, black vines; branching out from the lower right side of my spine, tentacles sprout all the way up to the back of my neck.

"You branded me, you son of a bitch." Sewn into my flesh, I take off my pajamas to see that the tendrils run down the back of my right leg, also.

"Oh god."

I no longer trust how well I'm feeling. This was the work of the beast.

"What is this? What did you do to me?"

The creaking of floorboards echoes into the bathroom. Following the noise, all the vegetation gently coils.

"Oh no, you don't! You're gettin' it!"

I spring out of the bathroom and through our bedroom. I'm not sure what I'm going to say or if I'm even that mad, but I need some kind of closure on my anatomy. If I were a little less fuming, I might even appreciate how nimble I am as I bound toward the stairs. The steps are free and clear, which makes me feel that the creature is more aware than it seems.

Good.

I want it to know that it can't just manipulate someone against their will, even if it's for the better. I clear my throat with a grunt. I try to assert some kind of bravado. It'll understand that even if it doesn't speak English.

Oh my. The creeping.

It wasn't the beast.

"Father."

"Oh! There you are. Apologies, once again, for the intrusion."

I know it's only been a day, but he looks exactly the same. He takes his hat off as soon as he sees me and starts fiddling with it in a twitchy, clockwise motion. A nervous tick, I guess.

He is trespassing in our home and at an unreasonable hour. I'm not what I used to be, but I do feel like I can wallop him if I have to.

"An open garage is one thing, Father."

"Rightly so, rightly so, but I was invited in," says the priest.

I look at our front door. It's wide open by the will of the overgrowth. The creature's reach has made it to the front door. I'm sure the warpath I left in the first-floor bathroom is now covered in life.

"It's not *its* house, and, I have to say, you don't seem very startled . . . " I trail off in what I hope is a threatening manner as I step to close the distance between us.

"Certainly, sir, certainly. An intrusion that lies entirely upon my person."

"And I don't know what time it is, but I do know it's not an appropriate time for visitors. Welcome or otherwise."

"I can leave, if you so wish."

"Maybe. What's up? What do you want?"

"I wanted to see to your well-being, sir. I've heard of your strife."

"Strife? What do you know about my strife?" My voice shakes, gurgling up from the pit of my gut. The verbal lashing I've been preparing for the beast is being dumped on my uninvited guest.

"I-I-I just see that you are in nee—"

"Who are you? What makes you think that you can keep barging in like this!"

I shove his shoulder, and his spirit wilts.

"Please, sir. I mean you no—"

"What do you actually want? Are you even a priest?"

"Yes, it's just-I heard—" He cowers backward as I step forward. I can feel the room tense and coil as I approach. I can wallop him.

"Heard? Who'd you hear it from? It sure as hell isn't the hospital."

I shove him again. He feels like a bird under his thick coat. Mostly bones.

Let's see if they're hollow.

"Huh? Answer me!"

I don't even have to push him this time around; one more aggressive step forward is all it takes for him to topple backward.

Panicked, he pulls his white collar off.

"Big surprise, not a priest."

I lift my foot to pin him down. Before my sole can come down on him, he pulls his shirt down to reveal his neck.

"Please, I am a priest, sir. I'm sorry. I'm sorry," the priest pleads, displaying his own black brands. He's been touched by the beast as well. They run up his neck and meet over his heart. I was embarrassed when I woke up this morning, and I'm embarrassed now. Why wouldn't he assume I was up to speed on the creature?

I get a taste of what it's like to be limber, and I immediately abuse it.

I've set a weird tone for the day.

"It's concerned," the priest continues, "worried, sad."

"Concerned?"

"Yes, indeed, sir."

"Concerned with what?"

"You."

Me?

I put my foot back down to the floor. After a long sigh, I look at my own tattooed hand and back to the priest. His eyes are closed tight, hoping the reveal will save him from any further punishment. The surrounding vines relax when I do.

"Coffee?" I ask him.

He's been quiet since I bullied him. He is fragile. There was barely any strength in his grip when I hoisted him up. Seeing him hunched over our kitchen island with a sheepish frown leaves a sinking feeling in my stomach. I deserve it, and I'm sure this coffee won't alleviate that feeling. I slide a mug over to him, and he nestles it, similar to how he nestles his hat. A hat he has put back on and has yet to take back off. I guess he sees it as some form of protection, even if it's just figurative.

"Oh, thank you," he squeaks, and that stings. He's still so cordial.

"So what happened there?" I ask as I motion to the flannel over my own chest. I was in a hurry, so I didn't think that the garish pairing of a blue and yellow flannel shirt with Christmas pants would be that offensive, but now that things have died down, it might be worse than the bullying.

"Miocardiopatía Dilatada Idiopática," he explains with a voice of silk.

"That's a mouthful."

"It's um, how do you word it, a round heart. Well, it used to be."

"Did it fix you?"

He sips our coffee. I hope he likes it. It's the first batch I made with a clear head. Well, clearer. A lot has been going on.

"Mmhm. I was born with it, so it is still a somewhat new . . . um, new feeling? Breathing the way I do. Clean."

"That must be quite a change."

"Remarkable. Remarkable change."

"Yeah . . . but the process is . . . that was something." I sip my own coffee. Damn, that is good. He has to like it.

"Terrifying. Certainly. Certainly, terrifying."

"That's for certain. I was trying to build a pond when I found it."

"A burial plot in my parish had to move because of it. When I investigated, something was alive. I thought it was a person."

"Where's your parish, Father?"

"Stella Maris. Cabo de Hornos."

"Sorry, I don't know it. Is that downtown? I don't go out much."

"Chile."

I almost do a spit take. "Wait, what?"

"Mmhm, It's a little island. Hornos. Horn. Cape Horn. I miss it. I miss it so."

"Chile. Like, South America?"

"And south for South America. Yes."

"Oh my, you've been on some journey."

"I have not been back for quite some time." He stares into his coffee with a longing that reminds me of what this house used to look like. Now a garden of its own, I offer more coffee to the young Priest. "Yes, please, sir."

"You can call me Ed." I pour the coffee in as his spirits seem to rise.

"Yes, thank you, sir Ed." Adorable.

"So there's more than one?" I ponder as I put the French press back in its flowered resting place.

"Mmm." He shakes his head as he sips his topped-off coffee. "No, no. There's just one. Everywhere it pops up is a part of the whole."

"What? No. It's not. Can't be."

"Very much so." The Priest holds out his hand, and the adjacent vines reach out and caress his fingers. "You can recognize a friend wherever you are in the world."

"But Chile to Oregon? That's insane."

"Uh, three sites in Brazil, one in Uruguay, one on the border of Colombia and Ecuador . . . "

"No, come on."

" . . . one off the coast of Japan. I'm confident there's at least four in China, but they will not have me in, but Nepal has the biggest one I have seen, Pakistan has two—"

"How long have you been traveling?"

"Two and half-three years now. It's difficult to say."

"But you said it recently healed your round heart?"

"When you are not able to stand and walk a few meters without rest since born, three years is new."

"That's fair. But how's it that . . . big?"

"The earth's center contains more than a quadrillion tons of gold. Entire oceans are hundreds of kilometers below our feet. Life on Earth is as old as the Earth itself, and the, um, ingredients of life have been around as long as anything. Every day, there are more people on the planet than there ever were, so there are more souls than there ever were, but those souls come from something. And those souls before us. We all started somewhere."

"You think it's as old as the Earth?"

"Older."

"How'd you come to that conclusion?"

"No, no. Nothing concludes. Life didn't start here, nor will it end here. Just like it, space is still stretching, so that means it was smaller so long ago. Less complex, you see. Space at one time was an . . . uh . . . what is the word I'm trying to . . . ?"

"Ecosystem?"

"Yes. At one time, space itself was its own oceans and forests and clouds and jungles and mountains. Ingredients closer together. A world older than religion."

"How do you feel about that, being a man of God?"

"God is the name we give the mystery. Our friend is just a beautiful clue. An earthling before we named it Earth."

No. That's too simple. It's a preposterous idea, but four days ago, digging up a self-animating root that would fix my bad back was a preposterous idea. It's something to consider, looking down at the wondrous simplicity of the tendril in my hand. It is laced with gold, after all.

"This coffee is quite nice."

Oh, thank god, or . . . the thing outback.

"Oh, good. Glad you like it."

"I'm glad you're well, Ed. It was worried."

"It was worried?"

"Mmhm. That's why I'm here."

"It can do that?"

"Why wouldn't it? We all have the same soul ingredients."

"I mean, it can communicate to you that I was— you know what? Sure."

I'm not getting into the metaphysics of the soul with a Priest. Especially one with more experience with the newly discovered organism. He'll have an answer for everything, and that's a recipe for an argument, even if with all the ingredients.

"That's comforting, I suppose." I say, after a moment.

"Very much so, sir Ed. Very much so."

"You don't have to call me sir."

"Certainly, Mr. Ed. Certainly." Ugh. He pushes his mug aside and stands up. He stretches his back and lifts his arms over his head. "Thank you for the coffee. Is there anything else you would like to discuss?"

Alex is the first thing that comes to mind, and I'm sure he'll have some comforting soliloquies relating to grief, but, "no, thank you, Father. I very much appreciate the visit."

"Until I see you again." He reaches his hand out.

"That sounds unlikely with your travels." I'm hesitant to shake since the last time we made contact was an assault.

"We most certainly will." His hand lunges toward mine, and he shakes it with a vigor I didn't believe he had. "Good day, Edward."

He puts his hat on and shuffles toward the front door. Gentle morning light washes over me as the house opens the door for the Priest.

Is this it? That felt too easy. Is this my last chance to get any answers? Where's he going now? How's he getting there? Does he really have answers or just whimsical thoughts? Maybe that's what you need to confront the impossible. He's gotten this far.

"Excuse me, sorry. One thing?"

"Yes?" He turns to me from the doorway.

"Why now? Why's it just starting to come to the surface?"

"Hard to speak for it, but if I had to, I'd be ready for something new."

"Okay . . . okay. Take care, Father."

"You as well."

Before he leaves, he pulls two berries off the vines hanging from the door frame.

ROOTS RUN DEEP

"Te agradecemos mucho." He speaks with it like I do.

He eats the green berries and dissolves into the rising sun. I bet those are nutritious.

As far as ambassadors to a new and potentially terrifying status quo go, I can't imagine a better one. Gentle, impartial, and just as confused as I am. He also has a genuine beast beyond comprehension to cite. He's the full, messianic package. We've also tended to swing toward anti-establishment, but this thing may be the first establishment. Hard to argue with that level of purity, especially with the centuries of convoluted human bullshit built on top of it. No wonder it wants to rinse and repeat.

Hm.

It.

Well, a primordial life form nurtured in fledgling spacetime comprised of the raw exploded debris from the Big Bang? Or, at least, an organism developed from life derived from life derived from spare parts of the origin of the universe. The odds of that seem incalculable, but then again, if that is what it is, then it's a physical certainty. It's just a matter of time. Then that would make *me* the incalculable phenomenon lucky enough to come across a cosmic inevitability. I'm the undiscovered critter from the mysterious world above.

Huh, 'lucky.'

It's hard to feel lucky walking up the stairs to no one. I'm not sure what to do with the rest of my day. I should probably start to consider how I'm going to live. If my friend is uprooting itself from the center of the Earth, modern civilization may be in for a rude awakening. It can move entire forests with little effort. It's hard to imagine what effort would look like.

Where does that leave me?

I don't think I want to see it. I couldn't and still don't imagine a future without Alex. Am I supposed to persist with an impending global ecological shift? I don't want to exist, in general, let alone during such a transition. It's already too much.

"Oh my . . . oh . . . "

Our bed.

This is our bed.

And there you are . . . were.

In our bedroom, the Earth has blossomed into a living memorial. Flowers and vines have taken the shape of Alex on her side of the bed. Gently nestled to the edge, with her hands folded under her cheek. She's resting in the same place she has for years. Next to me. With me. I've come to change out of my clashing outfit, but my legs weaken at the sight.

I sit on the edge of the bed. It's back to normal. I can feel her weight against my own. I have been in this position thousands of times in our life. I sat here before my route just to be here with her. It was so nice. I would wake up to get here. I would leave so I could get back here. I built a life just to relive this moment every day, and I did it. It was so peaceful. So lovely. How lucky I was. How lucky I am, to have known such a moment, to have lived it too many times to count. It's hard to imagine, but I hope I gave you the same.

It's not her. I know that, but I do cherish the opportunity to relive this little ceremony. When was the last time I cried? I'm not sure, but the tears I shed now seem bottomless, and I'm going to sit right here and find out if that's true.

THE LIVING ROOM

I'VE PACKED THE essentials with nowhere to go. My sixty-five-litre backpack is filled to the brim, ready to go by my feet, but has no destination in mind. As much as I'll miss our home, it'll be uninhabitable in a day or two. The electricity went out while I was upstairs, and I didn't realize it because my friend is supplying light and heat. Thank god I made coffee when I did. Hyrdo's still running, though, so I'm not in an immediate panic. I haven't eaten one of its berries yet, but it'll be hard to leave here if I'm provided shelter, warmth, and nutrition. Maybe that's what I'll do. Just let it swaddle me in the bones of my memories until the end. Then, it can use my body for fertilizer or spare parts of building materials or whatnot. There are worse end-of-life plans, I suppose. It also gives me an excuse to stop writing this note.

Dear Derek is all I've written down. I am still livid. It's the only thing left that puts me in a spiral. How dare he? Decades of friendship turned to decades of recontextualized regret. I hate him for that and really want him to know it. He can live out the remainder of his days haunted by his actions. That's what he deserves. He's been trying to get a hold of me . . . well, us. I don't even know where my phone is, and wherever that may be, it's dead.

Huh.

He may not even know Alex has passed. I finally get some more pen to paper.

I just want to say—

"Edward! Oh my god, Edward, are you in there?!"

Mia?

Oh no. I can't make her coffee. And an ancient sentient life form with which I've bonded has taken over the house. I guess I can't let her inside.

I exit the front door, and Mia looks as if she just witnessed a murder.

"Mia? How can I—what, um, are you okay?"

Standing in our driveway with a backpack slung over her shoulder, I watch her look past me in morbid awe. I step out of our house and am sure to close the door behind me. Can't let her see the state of things.

"Mia? What's up?" I get a few feet away from her before I turn to follow her gaze.

Oh.

I guess it's been some time since I've looked at our house from the outside.

The outside matches the inside; a house tangled within pulsating verdure. I've only ever seen it in the micro. The macro perspective is a tad more terrifying. It's alive, gently billowing at the speed of breath, revealing fractured glimpses of a home underneath. For the uninitiated, this must be quite a sight.

"What happened? Are you okay? When did . . . ?" She can't keep her eyes off of it, and a wave of embarrassment churns my stomach.

"It's, um, it's a fairly new predicament, but I am wrapping my head around it."

"Is it because of the sinkholes?"

" . . . what?"

"So, you haven't looked at the news in the last twenty-four hours?" Mia asks, while sitting on the same stool as the priest. They have very different postures. She's upright and compact, doing her best not to come in contact with the beast. I've had both ends of the spectrum, in terms of visitors, today.

"I've had a lot going on." I stand on the other side of

the kitchen island, similar to how we first met. I'm still anxious about the lack of coffee to offer her.

"I can see that, but the world's been . . . changing."

"I can also see that." I do a little ironic flourish at the world of vines around me. Mia, for good reason, is not amused.

"Um, sinkholes have been hitting the coast and seem to be creeping inward. I'm fine where I am right now, but that can change any minute. The destruction is . . . I don't know, unprecedented."

"Yeah . . . it's hard to imagine this isn't all related."

"Well, you can't stay here."

"I think I will."

"No, you can't. How?"

"It's our home."

"No, no, that's ridiculous. Come with me. I can take you somewhere. Family? Friends? You can stay with us for a few days until we figure it out."

"That's very sweet, and it really does mean a lot, but I've made up my mind."

"How can you think that? How are you going to live?"

"I'll make due. Always have."

"It . . . It's . . . it's not a good idea."

"I'm sure it isn't, but thank you for coming to check up on me."

"That's not exactly why I came here." Mia opens the backpack that she's had on her lap. "I just wanted to make sure you had this." She takes a small bronze oblong cylinder from her bag and places it on the kitchen counter.

I know what it is, but I have to ask.

"Is that, um—" This has caught me off guard, I admit.

"Yes. I thought you should have it as soon as possible."

"It's um, she's, um, it's smaller than I would have imagined."

"It was their most modest urn."

"Urn . . . it's an urn."

I place my elbows on the counter and lean in close, losing myself in its dull sheen.

"You're back home, love," I attempt to whisper, but *love* gets caught in the back of my throat. A high-pitched squeak frees the word and sentiment outside of myself.

"You're back . . . " I'm lost.

"What was she like?" Mia asks after a long and distant pause.

That's right.

I'm here.

This is happening.

"Um, Alex. She was—I found her on the couch in the living room."

"I actually meant what—"

I know what you meant.

Forgive me, but I need to get there.

"She was on the couch in the living room. Unconscious. She was breathing but unresponsive. Turns out it was an aneurysm. A twenty-seven-millimetre, mycotic cerebral aneurysm. I didn't know what that meant at the time, but it apparently meant a blood vessel was infected, and that caused the rupture. Um, she went into surgery immediately, and, um, it was pretty big, but the chances were decent. Then pneumonia set in, and she never recovered. Never woke up, really. She opened her eyes for a few seconds at a time. She tried to talk once, but it was so weak. That's when palliative care stepped in and made her comfortable. The whole thing happened in less than three days. I was just . . . you know . . . the day before I found her was unlike any other day."

"I'm sorry, Edward," Mia says. She must be a nice presence in the hospital. I wish I could have met her there. "It's good you were there with her."

"Yeah . . . yeah . . . it's just that, it's funny, you know, I found her in the same spot we've cuddled in for decades. Our schedules were really different, but there were a few hours in between when I'd be falling asleep on the couch and she'd be starting her day. I'd rest my head in her lap, and she'd fiddle with my hair until she left. I'd doze off to old reruns as the sun would set. When we retired, we just did that most of the time. It was hard to want to do anything else. Day after day, we'd be on that couch. Watching old movies, or just talking, or just bullshitting on our phones. I know it's not very ambitious, but I couldn't really ask for anything better. And almost every day, she'd say *this is the best*. And, I don't know if it really was, but if it were, then that would mean every day was . . . it means that every day was the best day of her life. Up until the end. That's gotta mean something, right? It was rough for a couple of days, at the end there, but it was after decades of the best days of her life."

"It sounds like it."

I can't even hear, Mia. I can't even hear my own words. They leave me so swiftly and simply.

"And at the time, I thought, you know, the *best* was the show that we were watching or the time of day or whatever, but you know, maybe it was because . . . you know . . . .because of me . . . I was there every time she said, so . . . maybe it was me . . . .maybe I gave her that."

"If only we all could be so lucky." Mia's posture, at some point, became more relaxed. Her face doesn't express it, however. Her eyes are glassed over, and her lips are taught at the edges. She had to fight to tell me that. It must be overwhelming to see the state of the house.

"Hm . . . lucky."

Am I?

I've tossed that word around my skull quite a bit this morning. I don't know if I am, but I want to go on and find out. Two days ago, I couldn't even imagine tossing anything around my skull. My brain was just static, dialed up to its absolute, unbearable limit.

Now, I can have thoughts.

Clarity.

I'm sure it'll come in waves, but, at least, I know it's possible.

"Would you please reconsider coming with me?" She zips up her backpack and begins her exit.

"I'm afraid I've made up my mind."

"Sure, fine. But I'm leaving my number." She grabs the pen next to Derek's note and jots her number down on the back of his letter.

I don't have the heart to tell her my phone's probably crushed under a toppled-over backhoe. I'm not getting my deposit back. I haven't been back there today. My friend could have eaten the excavator for all I know. I shimmy my way out of the kitchen to let Mia out, but the house starts to do it for me. I grip the door handle before she notices.

"Oh, thank you," Mia responds.

"No, no, thank you. Today was . . . today was something."

"It certainly was. Take care, Edward," she replies as she walks away. She's leaving with weight on her conscience. She's leaving a sad widow in a ravaged house in a ravaged world.

"You too."

I want to tell her something, but what? How do you prepare someone for something like my friend out back? It tried to open the door for her, so it's displaying some kind of compassion. It watched her listen to my stories and do her best to comfort me in the most trying time of my life. I've shown it kindness, and it's done so in return. It's fond of the priest, and it recognizes him across years and continents. It seems to be able to discern decency.

"Mia?"

"Yeah," she replies, a few feet away from her car.

"You'll be okay. Just keep being you."

" . . . right. okay." She responds through the side of her mouth, shakes her head, and gets into her car. She doesn't wave as she drives off, but I watch her disappear into the winding woodland. Not as wise or lyrical as I hoped to be, but my days have been full of hindsight, lately. Maybe she'll remember my attempts at eloquence when she meets it. Probably not. I might be a rambling, old coot from here on out, but she will be okay. The door opens for me as I walk back toward the house.

ROOTS RUN DEEP

"Sorry, but I don't think she's ready for you yet, but be a gentleman when she is." I step through the doorway.

"Oh my. Hey, love."

I walk up to the urn on the counter. I'm afraid to pick it up. It's just metal. Metal containing the remnants of the love of my life. Once I do, I'm aghast by how light she is. Shouldn't it be more? Shouldn't she leave something behind?

I guess she did. I'm still around.

Looking into the living room, I no longer see the teeth or claws that kept me away. But I can see our couch. What can this room possibly do to me now?

Carrying the Urn, I saunter into my favorite place on earth.

No matter where we've been, in all of our travels, we've never seen a place more lovely. There was no such place we'd rather be. There isn't! There isn't a better place, event, function, ceremony, or concert that's even rivaled the pure satisfaction that's taken place in this room. You haven't experienced a song as sweet, a drug as intoxicating, or sex as orgasmic. There have never been, or forever ever will be, experiences as fulfilling and pure and genuine as what has occurred in this room. And all we needed was a couch and each other.

The creature. It's done something to our garden. I step out back with Alex's ashes under my arm.

"Hey, what have you been up to?"

The giant serpent of the earth looms over a tunnel that gradually sinks lower and lower underground. It's massive and wide enough to fit a bus through.

"What'd you do?"

I step down into the pit, it's a bit easy to maneuver now, with the creature's aid. I stand by its circular, organic entrance.

Ohhhhhhhhh my . . .

There's a city under our home. There is no way to describe it other than that. The tunnel widens the further

~65~

down it goes and branches off to wider tunnels that branch off to wider tunnels. Its bulbs of golden and blue light stretch as far as I can see, with a sky of vines, walls of grass, and floors of moss. Water bubbles gently in pockets of valleys above my head and below my feet.

"What the hell—what is this?"

I look back down to the world unknown.

"Is this for me?"

✷✷✷

I took her spot this time around. Nestled in the corner where the armrest meets the pillow, I lean deeply into the living room couch. I don't need my friend's assistance this time around. It knows it as well, as the windows are clear of vines. It doesn't matter how early I am for sunset. I have every sundown that has come before it. If I don't get it now, I never will. Holding Alex, we stay to see the sun melt into the horizon and for the stars to take its place. It's time to get up shortly after they shine. I have what I need.

There's a fishnet cup holder outside of my backpack. Three water bottles are unnecessary, but Alex's urn needs a place.

Ah, shit. I was afraid I was forgetting something. Before I sling the backpack around my shoulders, I slide Derek's note close to me. Giving it a quick once over, I grab the pen Mia used. I can even see her phone number through the blank white paper. I sigh long and hard while my brow scowls at my newly acquired arch-nemesis.

Hate. I absolutely hate this. I write my note and march off in a huff. He better read it, that son of a bitch. I don't want a doubt in his mind. There's not a single misplaced word or fabrication.

Dear Derek, You are a cherished friend. Thank you for letting us know you. Love, Edward and Alex.

And I do.

It's harder to scale down into the pit this time around. It's no fault of the creatures'. I'm just on wobbly legs. I have never been this nervous and frightened. This monster was tearing me apart, and I wasn't this scared. The knot in my gut is so tight it feels like I swallowed a fist of ice.

Am I ready for this, or am I going to end up killing myself, sad and alone? Will there be other people down there? What will they be like? What if I get lost? Can I turn back? If I go down too far, will I be able to breathe? What if I become claustrophobic? It's not like there's a sky underground. Will I get enough vitamin D? I'm so old. Am I strong enough for something like this? Is my mind? What if I get injured or get hungry or have another panic attack?

I've never been this afraid. There are so many unknowns.

I just don't know what's going to happen.

You didn't before, Ed, but now you do. The literal worst thing you imagined happened. And you're still here. What else can you be here for?

Resting my head on the edge of the cave, I close my eyes and think of Alex.

"Show me something new, okay?" I ask the beast.

ACKNOWLEDGMENTS

For Chris. I'll keep trying, but so far, there is no collection of the 170,000 words I could coddle together to express my profound love and admiration.

I have joked with my husband about dying last. To avoid any more loss in his life, it's become a foregone promise that I'll be there to comfort their transition to the great mystery. Teehee, that's romantic. The problem is, that joke has reverberated throughout our lives enough that it has now become a melancholic goal. Dying after a loved one is a lofty sentiment, and as much as you try, death is unpredictable. That's the rub.

I've laid awake more times than I can count, dreading the day my father and dog, Cooper, died. They both died suddenly within six months, much sooner than anticipated, and I was the lone witness to their terminal incidents. I can't tell you if the nighttime dread primed my mind for the loss, but it was a miserable comfort to know I could get through it. I persisted and was present for their ends. That, in itself, was maturity by necessity. Shotgun therapy, if you will (go to actual therapy). *Roots Run Deep* is the first thing of mine my father will not read. So, a story about coming to terms with grief seemed apropos, but the self-reflection was what caught me off guard. Ultimately, it wasn't necessarily about processing grief but the indomitable preparation for moving forward.

One thing that does keep me awake that didn't before is my own death. Not because I fear the process of dying but of leaving loved ones behind. That immediate vacuum of loneliness is crushing beyond words. I can't imagine it's a healthy life goal, but the idea of dying last has become something of an ambition. It's even gone beyond my husband, and I now dream of being the last person I know. To ensure everyone I care for deeply has had someone by their side. Heady and wrought with martyrism, the forefront of my psyche knows it's silly but not silly enough to stop taking Omega-3 supplements. Maybe then, I can be my own comfort. But then again, why not while I'm still alive?

ABOUT THE AUTHOR

Finding high-school physics exceedingly difficult, Jason Krawczyk decided to pursue his passion for filmmaking. After shooting numerous music videos, commercials, and shorts, Jason directed his first feature-length project, "The Briefcase." In 2015 Jason wrote and directed the Henry Rollins horror-comedy "He Never Died," which premiered at South By Southwest and is currently streaming on Netflix. The sequel, She Never Died, was released in 2020 on Amazon Prime with his new project "Sunset Superman," starring Michael Jai White, premiering in 2024.

Along with directing, Jason Krawczyk has written, punched up, and ghostwritten several screenplays, novels, and novellas, with his first publication, "An Earth That Knows Magic," released in 2022 by Black Hare Press and "It Looks Like Dad" in 2023 by Little Ghosts Books with "Reality Squall" scheduled for release in 2024 by Nosetouch Press. His passion for writing led him to co-own Little Ghosts Books with his husband, Chris Krawczyk, an inclusive cafe and bookstore that offers readers horror books from sterling classics, LGBTQ authors, and burgeoning indie publishers.

Jason's primary goals are honing his writing, directing, and storytelling craft while collaborating with the talented people he has met along the way.

www.ingramcontent.com/pod-product-compliance
Lightning Source LLC
Chambersburg PA
CBHW011436240626
47153CB00011B/3016

MAX BOOTH III

THE 'DILLO

Ghoulish Ghosts
an imprint of Ghoulish Books & Little Ghosts Books
San Antonio, Texas | Toronto, Ontario

The 'Dillo

ISBN: 978-1-963801-07-1

www.GhoulishGhosts.com

Cover by Chris Krawczyk

For all the armadillos out there

for all the humanities out there

MY WIFE TOLD ME she was leaving. I said bullshit you ain't, she said bullshit I am. Why in the hell would she want to go and do that, I wondered. Wasn't I a good enough husband? Didn't I satisfy all her needs and desires? Didn't I provide for her?

"No," she said, arms folded across the kitchen table, "you're *not* a good enough husband, and you *don't* satisfy any of my needs *or* desires. Also, you don't provide *shit* for me."

"What the hell are you even talkin' about, woman," I said.

"You are a lousy drunk, Wayne."

"Bullshit." I hiccupped and raised my can of beer as a salute. "I'm a great drunk. One of the best. Ask anyone."

"Last week you couldn't even walk to bed. You broke all my grandma's china. Those were family heirlooms."

I shrugged. This lecture was bullshit. "That's what you get when you buy somethin' that wasn't manufactured in the U-S-of-A. *China*. Ha. Now that's a funny joke, all right. I oughta post that shit on Facebook."

"I've already talked to a lawyer. This is happening."

"The fuck's a lawyer gonna do? I'll fight any goddamn lawyer in Texas. Buncha pussies is what they are." I was reminded of a series of billboards I always saw around San Antonio that read GOMEZ LAW FIGHTS. Who was this Gomez, I often wondered, and where did these law fights take place?

"I can't keep living like this, Wayne. I deserve better."

"And what about me? What do I deserve?"

Tonya looked at me then with absolute pity. I didn't care for that look one bit. "That's not up for me to decide."

She got up to leave, and only then did I notice the multiple suitcases next to the kitchen door. All packed and ready to go.

"Wait!" I screamed. I tried to stand, but my legs were

weak and wobbly, so I collapsed back in my seat. "Be honest. This ain't about my booze at all, is it?"

She shook her head. "That's exactly what it's about."

"Nuh-uh," I said, shaking my head right back at her. "This is about that goddamn 'dillo, ain't it? You're pissed that I ain't killed it yet. That it wrecked up your garden."

She hesitated at the door, looking like someone with a secret to unload. "Wayne, there's somebody else."

"What do you mean, there's somebody else?"

"I mean, I'm in love with another man," Tonya said. "His name is Sebastian. He has an Amazon Echo. You can ask it any question in the world and it knows the answer."

"Baby, if you want an Amazon Echo, I can get you an Amazon Echo. All you had to do was ask."

She shook her head, disgusted by the mere sight of me. "They're like a hundred dollars, Wayne. You could never afford it."

I sunk back in my seat. She was right. That was way out of my budget. "What kinda questions you got that're so pressing you need them answered by some robot, anyhow?"

"You just don't understand, do you?"

"Understand *what*?"

"The whole point is, it's there if I need it. It's dependable. Sebastian takes care of me. He has an Amazon Echo. He has HBO Max added on to his Hulu account. He has one of those fancy coffee pots that only make one cup instead of a whole pot."

"What the fuck's so fancy about that? Why would you only want one cup?"

"Sometimes, that's all I have time for."

"So what? Just save the rest of the pot for later."

"But then it gets gross tasting, Wayne. You know that." Tonya started sobbing. "I can't do this with you anymore. Sebastian is waiting on me. We're going to watch HBO together and drink one cup of coffee each. He's way more of a man than you could ever be."

"But Tonya, come on, you don't mean any of this."

THE 'DILLO

"My lawyer will be in touch."

And then, just like that, she was gone.

I was alone in the house we'd been living in together for the last decade. The house I assumed we would both die in. I had this ongoing fantasy of us breathing our final breaths here—together, at the same time. Our bodies would decompose side by side until a neighbor finally complained about the smell. The city would have to bust down the front door with a battering ram. A team of dipshits in hazmat suits would get called in to investigate the situation. The news article would go viral online with a headline that would be whacky and sensational. I thought about this often, usually while on the toilet or in bed when I had trouble going to sleep.

Our house. Except . . . now it was just *my* house. Tonya had left. She didn't want the house anymore. She didn't want me anymore. Our marriage was over. Our life together had come to an end.

And it was all because of that goddamn 'dillo.

I grabbed another beer from the fridge and headed out to the front yard to kill that sumbitch once and for all.

The thing you need to understand about the 'dillo is it was a piece of shit and I hated it.

It first started making our lives miserable about a month before Tonya left me.

Digging its stupid, ugly snout into our precious dirt and making a mess out of everything. Tonya had this garden, see, she'd grow these tomatoes as big and round as her tits—the 'dillo destroyed those, too. Not her tits. The tomatoes. Destroyed the whole goddamn garden. Now I'd never get to feast on her tomatoes again. Or her tits, for that matter. If I'm being honest, both went pretty great with a little mayonnaise spread across them.

Tonya said, Wayne, you gotta do something about this!

I loved those tomatoes! But I was pretty tired when she told me this, so I said I'd take care of it the next day. Well, the next day came and I got too busy watching professional wrestling on the TV, so it just didn't happen. And the longer I procrastinated with this chore, the uglier our front yard got, which I honestly didn't mind too much considering who gave a shit about front yards, anyhow? It wasn't fucking up the TV or drinking my booze, so what did it matter? But Tonya didn't see it that way. She wanted me to be a man. What's being a man got to do with anything? I wondered, and she said real men protected their women from mischievous armadillos. Maybe she had a point. I don't know. I was pretty drunk at the time and don't remember a lot of the conversation.

But now she was gone and there was no use ignoring the biggest problem in our lives. The thing that destroyed our marriage and ruined everything.

"Come on out, you fuckin' communist libtard," I shouted from my front porch. "I got your unabomber manifesto right here in my dickhole." I grabbed my crotch for extra emphasis. The 'dillo was nowhere in sight, but that didn't mean anything. It was clearly intimidated by my presence and hiding, waiting for me to return inside so it could continue wrecking my front yard. Well fuck that. I wasn't going nowhere. I had everything I could possibly need out here. I had my beer. I had my shotgun. I had my sunflower seeds. If I had to piss, I'd just water the grass and fantasize about the 'dillo slurping some of it up next time it passed through. As far as shitting, well, I wasn't a complete animal. I could wait until sundown before squatting behind a bush.

I'd even rolled out the TV to keep me company. If anything, the bunny ears antenna picked up a stronger signal without the roof of our house getting in the way. That night, I got good and drunk while watching professional wrestling on my porch TV. It was decent inspiration for what I could do to the 'dillo once I got my

hands on it. Assuming I didn't blow it away with the shotgun first, of course. If I got the chance to snatch it up that would be my go-to plan. I wanted this thing to feel pain. It did not deserve a slow death. I wanted to chokeslam it off of my porch. If 'dillos even had necks. I didn't know much about their anatomy, truth be told. But that was okay. If the fucker didn't have a neck, I could do other things. Body slams. Drop kicks. I'd give the little sumbitch the iron claw, if it came down to it.

Then, after I'd taken care of this yard pest, I'd go find my wife's lover Sebastian and pile-drive him through his fancy Amazon Echo. I'd get his arm in a lock so fierce he'd be begging for mercy, but would I let go? No sir. Not until I heard the bone snap.

I would wrestle anybody and anything that got in the way of winning Tonya back into my good graces. We were married, goddammit. My uncle—an ordained minister and fishing bait and tackle proprietor—had officiated the ceremony his own self. We had recited vows to each other. We had made promises. And to throw it all away, for what? For the armadillo-free residence of another man? I'm sorry but that was just cowardly. Had she always been so yellow? I couldn't recall. I like to think she had more of a spine when my uncle married us behind his bait and tackle shop. In fact, I know she did, because that was the very same afternoon Tonya had also buried her elbow in the hood of a cop car for daring to give us a parking ticket on the day of our wedding. And that hadn't even been the first time I'd seen her do something crazy like that. So what had happened since then? What had softened her up? Was I truly the one responsible for her gradual decline into becoming a total pussy? I refused to accept that. I was still the same man she'd married. I hadn't changed outside of maybe becoming even more of a badass. I had a tattoo now. That was definitely new. It was the shape of Texas, located directly upon my heart. Tonya didn't have any tattoos. She didn't have shit.

She'd claimed my boozing drove her away, but we both

5

knew that was a boldfaced lie. She drank just as much as I did, if not more so. Alcoholism was one of the things we most had in common. I mean, for crying out loud, hadn't we met in a bar? Hadn't the first question I ever asked her been, "Say there, fine thing, you mind buying your fellow American something to wet his whistle on?" Had she told me to go fuck myself back then? Had she lectured me on the health status of my fuckin' liver? Of course not. She'd giggled and asked what I was having, and I'd said, "Well, I'd love a sampling of what's between those two thighs of yours, but for now I reckon a Lone Star will do just fine." And had she purchased me not one but *three* Lone Stars after that, at each one somehow wiggling closer and closer to my stool until our knees were touching? And had I indeed ended up sampling the sweet nectar between her thighs that very night? I don't recall hearing a single complaint. Not then and not during the majority of our marriage. Not one utterance of negativity.

Until that fuckin' armadillo announced itself upon our property by destroying the little tomato plants she'd spent all summer fussing over. After that, suddenly she was full of complaints. About me, about everything. I drank too much. I watched too much professional wrestling. I spent too much time with my uncle. I didn't take her garden seriously. I didn't respect our lawn. I didn't know how to hunt armadillos. Yada yada yada. Oh, I'm sorry if I worked all day and wanted to kick back and relax a little when I got home. Suddenly it was a crime to drink a beer and watch professional wrestling on the TV I paid for with my own hard-earned money. It wasn't Amazon Echo money, but it was enough to live a perfectly content life together. What happened was she got greedy. This Sebastian fucker gave her a taste of delicacy, and now she was hooked—bait, line, and sinker, as my uncle would say.

Well, I'd show them all, goddammit. And I'd do it while drunk off my ass, too. Prove once and for all that alcohol wasn't a problem—it was a solution.

The 'dillo came that night, just as I'd expected. It couldn't resist taunting me. Rubbing it in my face. It wanted me to admit that it had won and I had lost. The same thing Tonya wanted me to admit. Everybody wanted me to surrender. This whole goddamn miserable universe was rooting against me. I wouldn't. I *couldn't*. Once a person gave up, there was no coming back. There was no returning to any previous perception of normality. They'd just continue freefalling in a state of decline until there was nowhere else for them to go but six feet under.

Well, I wasn't ready to do that.

I was gonna fight for what was mine. I was gonna get it all back and then some. I was gonna *win*.

I heard the little bastard before I saw it. Scuttling around Tonya's garden bed, flinging dirt haphazardly. At first I thought I was dreaming. The TV was still on, but wrestling was over and now some steak knife infomercial was playing. I turned it off and slowly stood up, then crept across the porch with my shotgun pointed straight ahead, finger already curled around the trigger and eager to blow this abomination to smithereens.

Right away I realized one of the flaws in my plan. There weren't any lights out here. I peered over the porch railing but I couldn't see shit. It was pitch-black outside. Not a soul except for me and the 'dillo were awake at this hour. The street was bare and the wind was still. Almost like time itself had frozen in place. I apologize for getting all poetic but sometimes a fella can't help it.

I could still hear the fucker, though. I detected the dark outline of a bush shaking back and forth. If I focused hard enough, I could also make out the faint glow of its shell vibrating within the foliage. It was somewhere in there, wreaking havoc. This would be the last bush it ever molested. I aimed the shotgun and

sucked in a breath and fired. The night erupted with the boom of my firearm. Something flew up from the bush and I realized too late that I was staring at the 'dillo jumping straight into the air. *Had I hit it?* I ran around the porch and descended the steps, then hustled across the yard toward the garden.

"I got you now!" I shrieked. "I got you now!" But there was no sight of it. The sumbitch had done leapt into a whole other universe.

Then, behind me, on the street: the pitter-patter of its tiny toes as it fled on the pavement. I spun around with the shotgun ready but I was too late. The 'dillo was already halfway down the block, illuminated only by the lampposts it fled under and the pink glow that radiated from its enigma of body armor. I gave some consideration into chasing after the 'dillo, but noticed several of my nosy-ass neighbors had started turning their lights on and opening their front doors to investigate the commotion. I'm sure they would have understood the situation had I explained it to them, but by then I was in no mood to converse, so I gathered my stuff and fled into the house before any of them could confront me.

Forty-five minutes later, a cop car pulled into my driveway. The siren wasn't on, but its headlights still splashed across the living room wall across our front window. My first thought wasn't *cop,* though. It was, *Finally Tonya has come to her senses.* Imagine my disappointment when I peeked outside and spotted some Dudley Do-Right motherfucker creeping up my porch.

I didn't want to give him the satisfaction of knocking on my door, so I made sure to swing it open seconds before his fist could connect. The dweeb took one look at me and immediately drew his firearm.

"Sir, put down the weapon," he said, voice trembling.

"What weapon?" I asked, two seconds before remembering that I was still holding the shotgun. "Oh, yeah, my bad." I tossed the shotgun on the couch, and the

cop flinched like it might go off and blow off his pecker. I couldn't help but let out a little giggle after imagining that.

"Sir, is there something amusing you'd like to share with me?"

I thought about telling him what I was visualizing, but figured there was some Obama-instated law against fantasizing about police officer castration, so I shook my head and said, "Nah." Then I spit a glob of phlegm out on the porch, barely missing his foot, and asked him why the hell he'd decided to disturb me at such an ungodly hour. He grimaced at the spit, but otherwise didn't let on like the action had bothered him, which told me everything I needed to know about this particular man. He was spineless, and I would be able to control him like a little puppet if it came down to it.

"Well, sir," he said, "we received a couple calls tonight about a disturbance."

"What kind of disturbance?" I asked, although the way I said it, it came out as less of a question and more of a challenge.

"Uh, a gunshot kind of disturbance. Folks reported something loud going off. Like maybe, uh, a shotgun."

We both glanced over at the shotgun on my couch, then I looked him straight in the eyes and said, "I don't know anything about that."

"Sir?" the cop said, clearly baffled at how to proceed here.

"What's your name?" I asked.

"Sir?"

"Your name is sir?"

"No, sir." The cop cleared his throat. "My name is Officer Plank. Official Sebastian Plank."

Suddenly I was the one who'd forgotten how to speak.

"And what is your name?" the cop asked.

"Sebastian?" I muttered.

His eyes widened. "Whoa. It's not often I meet another Sebastian."

"Your name is Sebastian?" I said, feeling a rage pump through me that I hadn't experienced in at least an hour.

"Well, yes sir, but I reckon you ought to call me Officer Plank."

I leaned forward and he took a step back. "You don't happen to have an Amazon Echo—do you, Sebastian?"

"A . . . a what?"

"An Amazon Echo."

Sebastian let out a nervous laugh. "Oh, yeah. I mean, not on me. But at my house. Yeah, I got one of those. Why? Are you in the market for one?"

"What about HBO Max, Sebastian?"

"Wh-what?"

I leaned closer. My fists gripped the door frame so tight I was convinced the plaster was about to crack. "Do you, or do you not, have an HBO Max subscription?"

"Well, sir, it's just Max now."

"Excuse me?" I said, fully prepared to rip this fucker's head off.

"They changed the name," the cop explained. "They got rid of the HBO part."

"What the fuck are you talking about?"

"The app—it's just Max now."

"Just Max?" I said.

"Yessir."

"Well, that's the stupidest fucking thing I ever heard."

He shrugged. "I do like revisiting *Game of Thrones* every now and then. I don't even care what folks say online. That last season ain't too bad at all."

"Sebastian?"

"Yessir?"

"Are you fucking my wife?"

"Sir?"

"Are. You. Fucking. My. Wife."

The cop hesitated, then cleared his throat. "I'm afraid I don't read you, sir."

"How about this?" I said. "Unless you got a warrant,

you best get off my property before I shoot your ass for trespassing."

His face paled like he was going to be sick. "Sir, you can't shoot a cop."

"I can shoot whoever the hell I want," I told him. "This is still America, ain't it?"

"But there are laws, sir!"

I shook my head. He wasn't getting it. "Laws go out the window," I said, "the moment you steal another man's wife with Amazon Echoes and Just Max subscriptions." I cracked my neck. "Now, you gonna git? Or am I gonna have to make you git?"

He must have finally realized I meant business, because he scrambled back to his car and booked it out of my driveway. I recollected my shotgun and sat out on the porch for another hour, waiting for him to return with the cavalry, but nobody showed back up. It was as I figured. The man my wife had left me for was made of pudding. I wonder what she would have said if she'd witnessed our interaction tonight. Would she have still been hypnotized by his fancy gadgets, or would she have snapped out of it and returned home where she belonged?

I fell asleep thinking about the whole thing. When I woke up, I'd pissed my pants. They'd been my favorite pants, too. Instead of washing them, I simply threw them away and decided to forget they'd ever existed. While dragging my trash can to the curb, I thought, *This is a metaphor for something*, but I couldn't quite figure out for what. Also, I wasn't one-hundred percent positive what a metaphor was, exactly. I figured I had enough of an idea, though, and this was definitely one of them. *Fuckin' metaphors*, I thought, as I walked back to the house, *they're all over the goddamn place, ain't they?*

I didn't forget about the 'dillo. I was more determined than ever to erase it from existence. If the previous night had proven anything, it was that I'd been too relaxed about my goals. Maybe armadillos weren't as dumb as I'd initially believed. Killing this thing would not be as simple as blasting a shotgun from my porch. I'd have to execute a proper hunt. Something that involved forming a legitimate plan. So that's what I did.

First I took a shower to wash away the leftover piss. My thigh had gotten sticky and if there's one sensation I cannot abide, it is stickiness. Plus, it was starting to smell. I didn't want Tonya coming back home only to leave again because the house reeked of urine. Whether she believed it or not, I was a responsible adult. I could clean. I could bathe. I wasn't no goddamn baby.

While showering, I also jerked off, but that was unrelated to the pissing myself thing.

After getting dressed, I brewed a pot of coffee and fried up a couple eggs. I sat at the kitchen table eating and thinking.

What did I know about armadillos? Not a lot.

I didn't know much about any animal, to be honest. Growing up, we never had much use for pets. I never understood everybody's fascination with keeping wild creatures in their houses. They were meant to stay outside in nature. Let them fend for themselves and the most determined would survive. After all, ain't that how man came to conqueror the planet? Always felt a little pathetic, truth be told, the way people treat their dogs and cats and whatever the hell else. Dressing them up in clothes and tucking them into bed like they're children or some shit. How far has our species fallen? Not me, though. And not Tonya, either. She never gave a goddamn about having no tamed critters. There was a reason *pets* was a word scramble of *pest*. Just one of the many beliefs we shared. I wondered what Officer Sebastian Plank thought about animals. The way he'd presented himself last night, I

wouldn't have been surprised to learn that he had one of those little purse dogs. I bet he even brushed its teeth every night and gave it a little kiss on the nose. Pervert behavior, you ask me.

So what, realistically, *did* I know about armadillos?

I knew they made for great road kill. Before this particular 'dillo decided to invade our land, I had never seen a live one in person—only flattened, decayed corpses alongside I-35. So, like most living things, they were vulnerable to motor vehicles traveling at break-neck speeds. This didn't really help me with my specific situation, unless I planned on driving my pickup across the lawn, potentially straight into the front of my house.

They also seemed to be nocturnal. I hadn't caught a glimpse of my 'dillo while the sun was still up, so I assumed it slept during the day. Where was it resting, though? Must've been somewhere nearby for its constant terrorizing of my property to have continued so long. I heard once chickens slept in bushes. I wondered if the same was true for armadillos. Except chickens weren't nocturnal. If something tried sleeping in a bush in the middle of the day, they'd probably be pretty easy to spot. Plus humans didn't eat armadillo. As far as I knew, humans didn't eat *anything* nocturnal. Not enough vitamin D in their meat. So I guess chickens and armadillos couldn't have been less alike if they'd tried.

After some thought, I came to figure they probably slept in burrows. All my 'dillo seemed to do was dig up dirt. Literal dirt, I mean. Not juicy gossip or anything. It made sense that was how they slept, too. I wondered if it had a burrow in my own front yard that it'd claimed for a bedroom. Could it have been as simple as sticking my shotgun into every hole in my yard and pulling the trigger? How long would it take before Officer Sebastian Plank showed back up investigating another noise complaint?

If not the shotgun, then what about good old-fashioned fire? Pour some gasoline in each hole and strike a match.

Of course, I wasn't exactly the most knowledgeable when it came to gas lines. What if I accidentally blew up half the neighborhood? Tonya would definitely never take me back, if I were to do something stupid like that.

Did 'dillos *eat* dirt? Or were they only flinging it back and forth? I wasn't no man of science but I wasn't so sure dirt was edible for any species. Insects, then. They probably were eating insects, right? Ants and shit like that. Perhaps the solution to all of my problems consisted of planting little deadly scorpions in Tonya's torn-up garden. But what if one of them made their way inside the house? Dealing with an asshole armadillo was painful enough, but adding little deadly scorpions to the mix? Felt like a recipe for disaster that I wasn't prepared to confront.

What else did I know about armadillos? Based off last night, they could jump. I knew they had shells—or, at least, *some type* of protective casing. I thought maybe they could roll into a ball but couldn't remember if I was mixing that up with another animal. I knew not to touch them with my bare hands, that they were known for carrying diseases from medieval times. Not the family dinner theater attraction. I mean the actual historical period. Leprosy and shit like that. Unless they also got leprosy at the family dinner theater attraction. I couldn't see how that would have been good for business, though. Sometimes realism can go too far and turn the table against a fella.

What even *was* leprosy? I wasn't sure. I thought maybe it melted your skin off until you were just a walking skeleton, but I wasn't no expert. Either way, it was probably in my best interest to avoid physical contact. I doubted Tonya would still be attracted to me without any flesh. She could be shallow like that sometimes. But that was okay. I could understand a turnoff like that. I wouldn't want to fuck a skeleton, either. It could be hard to emotionally connect with someone who was just bones.

After finishing up my coffee and eggs, I figured it was late enough in the afternoon to crack open a beer. Booze

always helped me concentrate. When I was sober, I couldn't think for shit. The world didn't make much sense to me without being a little buzzed. As if to prove it, all it took was two cans of Lone Star before an idea started to form. After another three, I'd concluded that this idea would be the only way to proceed. I suppose I could reveal what the idea was right now, but wouldn't that ruin the suspense of the whole thing? Instead, let's keep that in my back pocket.

First I had to get my shoes on, then find the keys to my truck. This took nearly a half hour. The keys were easy to recover, as they were right where I always left them: stashed in a ceramic football on the coffee table. But my shoes, somehow they'd ended up in the bathtub. I must've taken a shower with them still on, because they were drenched. I picked one up and gave it a squeeze and a stream of water sobbed out of the sole. These were my only shoes. Most Texans also had a pair of boots, but I could never find a pair of affordable boots that fit me. I'd been cursed with wide, flat feet—a Texan's greatest shame.

I laid out my wet shoes on the porch in a patch of direct sunlight, then returned to the living room and plopped down on the couch with the last can of beer from the case I'd purchased at the beginning of the week. On TV, there wasn't much on. The news was saying something about liberals fixing another election. Big surprise there. I did some more channel surfing. There were a few game shows on, some judge shows. Sometimes I liked checking out those judge shows, just to see what petty shit people were suing each other over.

I'd never sued anybody in my life, and nobody had ever sued me. I wouldn't even know how to obtain a lawyer if push came to shove. Would I have to mail somebody a letter? I couldn't stomach the thought. Someone like Officer Sebastian Plank, I bet he had plenty of experience taking people to court. It was exactly the kind of spineless behavior that slimy sumbitch would excel at. I wondered

if he would try suing me, once Tonya returned to her senses and came back home. Well, let him go ahead and try. I would not hesitate to countersue him with an ass full of buckshot. Not a judge in the state would convict. Folks in Texas, we prided ourselves on the sanctity of marriage, unlike other miserable pissholes such as California or Austin.

I must've dozed off while watching one of the judge shows, because suddenly my neck ached and I was soaked with sweat the way I often got after napping on the couch. A rerun of *Home Improvement* was on TV now. Tim the Tool Man Taylor. Now there was an American. Sometimes in the shower I practiced imitating that growl he always did on the show, but I was never any good at it—certainly not confident enough to try impressing Tonya or anything. It was a private thing I did. Something just for me. Men and women, they need their privacy. This is why bathrooms are such sacred places.

I was hoping my shoes were dry by now, since one of the most essential parts of my plan involved a trip to the grocery store, so I headed back out to the porch to check on their current condition. If I'd exited my house a mere three seconds earlier, I might've had a chance at preventing what I was about to witness. But I didn't exit three seconds earlier. That's not what happened.

Instead, I stepped out onto the porch just in time to spot one of my shoes scurrying across the front yard. At first I obviously assumed it was moving by itself, perhaps with the guidance of some sort of supernatural presence inhabiting the fabric. But then the reality of the situation dawned on me. My shoe was being carried. Not by a hand but by a mouth.

The mouth of an armadillo.

Its two tails seemed to taunt me as it trotted away from the house.

By the time I recovered my shotgun from the living room, it was already gone.

The remaining shoe still wasn't dry. If anything, it'd only gotten wetter. I wondered if the 'dillo had pissed on it while stealing its companion. I wouldn't have put such a conniving act past that devious little fucker. Either way, there was no time to wait around for it to dry. I had places to be—places, unfortunately, that advertised strict NO SHOES NO SERVICE policies. It'd be interesting to find out whether they intended on enforcing the pluralization of that word—*shoes*.

To be on the safe side, I made sure to at least put a sock on the unlucky foot before heading on over to the grocery store. Unfortunately, I realized far too late that there was a huge hole in the sock, allowing my big toe to stick out in the open. I had already entered the grocery store when I made this discovery, which was also when I learned how dirty and jagged my toenails had become in Tonya's absence. She usually trimmed them for me. Not because I asked her to. It was something she wanted to do. Same thing when it came to popping my zits. In fact, she'd become infuriated with me if I tried popping them myself, like I was betraying her in some way. There was a kind of sexual thrill in it for her that I refused to analyze. It wasn't like I never benefited from any of this stuff, too. It wasn't like I also wasn't secretly turned on letting another person squeeze pus from my body and remove the nails from my fingers and toes. Humans are confusing creatures defying simple explanation. I'd long found peace with this truth. Could Tonya's new lover, Sebastian, have said the same? Somehow I doubted it.

At least I knew what I needed at the store. There would be no dillydallying today. First, I went for the essentials: beer and potato chips. After both were secured, it was time to collect the items I'd need to trap the 'dillo. This meant

heading over to the pet section—specifically, the dog area. I'd never had a dog in my life but I imagined they weren't too far off from armadillos. I was basing this off of nothing besides instinct, which had never failed me in the past.

I tossed a couple squeaky toys into the cart. None of them, sadly, were armadillos. Believe me, I looked. One was a rubber chicken. The other one was a giant plush ice cream cone. Neapolitan, by the looks of it. There was nobody else in the aisle, so I gave the fabric a little lick. It didn't taste like anything. I wondered if this was going to be realistic enough to trick a armadillo. I then wondered if armadillos were even familiar with the concept of ice cream in the first place. Who would have told them?

I kept the plush ice cream cone in the cart, anyway. There was something about it that I admired. I considered adding a box of dog treats, but figured they were too large for an animal used to sucking up bugs. Suddenly struck with inspiration, I approached a nearby employee and inquired about what kind of live insects they kept in stock. The grimace of disgust on her face was all the answer I needed, but still I waited for a verbal response. "We ain't got none," she said, and I nodded and went about my business.

Before leaving the store, I added the following items to my shopping cart: a jingle bell necklace, a steel cage for small animals, and another box of shotgun shells.

Fortunately the woman who rung me up was not the same person who I'd interrogated about live insects. I suspected they might've communicated before my arrival at the cash register, however, because she kept giving me a similar look as the other one had not ten minutes prior.

I wondered if they had any idea what I intended to do. I even asked them. I said to the cashier, "What do you think I'm gonna do with all this?"

And you know what she said to me? She said, "Mister, I don't want to know."

I didn't go home right away. My errands weren't completed just yet. Next I got myself some lunch from Burger Boy. Ate it out in the parking lot with one of the beers I'd bought from the grocery store. I propped my phone up on the dashboard and tried to watch YouTube videos of classic professional wrestling matches, but the signal was pathetic and the stream kept failing to properly buffer. There was a Burger Boy WiFi hotspot, but I couldn't guess the password. I tried 'burger.' I tried 'boy.' I tried 'burgerboy.' I didn't try anything after that. I'd finished my lunch by then and it was time to go.

My uncle's bait and tackle shop wasn't too far from the grocery store. I figured if any place in this godforsaken town sold live insects it would be here. There was only one vehicle in the parking lot, a pickup truck that hadn't been washed in at least a decade. There was a bumper sticker on the back of the truck's bed that said EVERY TIME YOU HONK AT ME THE COWBOYS LOSE ANOTHER SUPER BOWL. This was my uncle's truck. He'd been driving it ever since I was a little kid. I parked next to it and made my way inside, comforted that there wouldn't be any other customers to eavesdrop on our conversation. In fact, in all the years that I'd been coming here, I'd never seen another person shopping. How could he afford the rent? How could he afford the bait? And, for God's sake, what about the tackle? Surely it wasn't cheap to keep all of that in stock. But what did I know? My wife had left me and an armadillo had stolen one of my shoes. I wasn't much of an expert on anything these days.

My uncle was at the back of the store watching something on his laptop. To get there, I had to maneuver around several stacks of fishing rods that'd fallen over at least five years ago. At this point he probably viewed it as a

game to see how long he could go without having to pick them up. It didn't seem like the kind of game where you could win something—but, at the same time, what was there to lose? On his laptop he was watching YouTube clips of trains crashing into vehicles stalled on tracks. He was always watching videos like that. Once I asked him what he found so appealing about them, and he told me videos like that put hair on his chest. No further questions came to mind.

"Wayne, my nephew!" my uncle said when he saw me. He waved me forward, but did not pause the laptop or lower its volume, which must've been at full blast. We practically had to scream over the disturbing, grating sounds of total obliteration.

"How are you doing, Uncle?" I screamed.

"What was that, Nephew?" he screamed back.

"I said, how are you doing!"

"Oh, it's new, thank you!"

Frustrated, I leaned over the counter and lowered the laptop's volume. He glared at me like I'd just committed a war crime, and maybe that was true. There was no turning back now, though.

"I need bugs," I said. "Live bugs."

"Bugs I got," he said, clearly still pissed off at my act of betrayal. "What kinda bugs you after?"

"Whatever's gonna catch a 'dillo's attention."

He raised his brow, intrigued. "You hunting a 'dillo?"

"I ain't got much of a choice anymore," I told him. "Tonya done and left me."

My uncle blushed and inched closer to the counter, all conspicuous, and whispered, "She left you for an armadillo?"

"Not *for* one. *Because* of one."

"I'm afraid I don't follow, Nephew."

I sighed. I didn't come here to dump exposition. "We got one that's been causing a ruckus in her garden. She kept telling me to take care of it. I promised I would and then didn't. She implied I was an alcoholic and then moved into another man's house."

"Another man? What man?"

"A goddamn police officer," I told him. "Has an Amazon Echo and everything."

"Bullshit," my uncle said. "Ain't nobody around these parts can afford one of those."

"Well, evidently he can."

"On a cop's salary? Ain't no way." He licked his fingers, thinking it over. "Unless he's dirty."

"Name one who's clean."

"Dirty Harry."

I laughed. "His name is literally *dirty*, you fuckin' crackpot. Now you got them bugs I asked about or what?"

He gave me a real serious look and said, "Oh, I got bugs, all right. You can bet your sweet lily ass on that."

By the time I departed my uncle's bait and tackle shop, I had acquired an entire bucket overflowing with dirt and various insects. Worms, ants, beetles. I asked my uncle if we ought to separate them, in case one should murder the others before my return home, and he said, "God don't go about separating the earth, does she?" And I supposed he made a point there, so I nodded and told him to have a good night, then climbed back into my truck. I rested the bucket of bugs in my passenger seat and secured it with the seatbelt.

"Don't go making a mess in here, you understand?" I said to the bucket. "I got no time or inclination to clean up a mess right now. So, you just think about that."

And, goddammit, it must have understood what I said, because that bucket didn't move a lick my entire drive home. I should also mention that I was about four beers deep by then and usually when I was that far into my drinking I tended to speak to inanimate objects. But that was okay. As long as they didn't answer me, I wasn't fit for the looney bin. At least that's what my refrigerator always told me.

Okay, so, the plan.

First I must caution that it wasn't very clever, or complicated, but that was never my intention. I just wanted to get the job done. I wanted the armadillo out of my fucking life and Tonya back in it. You've probably already guessed at what I had in mind, and you'd be correct. Why else would I have purchased a dog cage, right? Or the insects, for that matter. The shotgun shells, in retrospect, also held a pretty predictable role. But that was okay. There was nothing wrong with predictability. There were plenty of things wrong in this world but predictability was not one of them. A person could depend on predictability. I'd heard that in a commercial once. A commercial for toilet paper, if my memory wasn't failing me—and why would it be? I was in the prime of my life. I woke up every morning with a hardon. My bowel movements always departed unobstructed. I seldom woke up screaming from an existential crisis. My body never required water. I had a perfect memory.

The first thing I did was set up the cage near Tonya's desecrated garden. I propped open its gate with a branch I'd torn from a neighbor's tree and tied a rope to it. The other end of the rope slithered across the yard up onto the porch, which was where I'd be hiding from sight while watching televised professional wrestling. Don't ask me where I got the rope from. Sometimes people just have things and there's no explanation for them. This was one of those.

Inside the cage I'd dumped the entire bucket of dirt and insects. Then I took a single can of beer from my new stock and poured it into the mound. I did this for a couple reasons. For one thing, didn't it prove a symbolic point against Tonya's insistence that booze had ruined my life?

THE 'DILLO

Would an alcoholic be able to willingly give up one of his beers to a pile of dirt? I think not. But on a more practical note I thought it might make it harder for the bugs to escape. Also, I had it in my head that the 'dillo would find the alcohol irresistible, and quickly get too drunk to put up much of a fight upon its capture. I reckon some of the bugs immediately drowned, the ones that couldn't handle a party. But others seemed to thrive. These were the cool bugs. I liked them the best. Created my very own little ecosystem in this cage, is what I did. Honestly made me feel a little jealous that it was all for the armadillo, that I couldn't fit inside of the contraption and . . . well, not live there, but at the very least socialize.

Before leaving the yard, I tossed the squeaky toys into the cage, too, and watched a swarm of undefinable insects inspect them from every angle. It was reassuring to know that even if the 'dillo ended up possessing zero interest in a rubber chicken, or a fake neapolitan ice cream cone, at least the bugs from my uncle's bait and tackle shop found them intriguing enough. I did wonder how much of that was the alcohol in their system, though. Would they have cared about the rubber chicken so much if they'd been sober? Would they have still mistaken the neapolitan as legitimate? Sometimes questions like these plague me. There are simply no good answers.

With everything set up to the best of my capabilities, I settled in on the porch with my beer and potato chips. The television was on, but at a low volume. I didn't want the extreme noises of professional wrestling to accidentally spook away the armadillo. Not this time. This time, I wanted it to feel nice and welcome. I wanted it to feel at home. I double-checked my shotgun was loaded, and wondered how big of a mess the gunshot would make. I smiled, thinking about it, and reminded myself to take a photo of the aftermath for Tonya once we'd reconciled.

Three beers later, I dozed off in my chair, and only stirred awake to the distant sound of slurping.

At first, the noise puzzled me. But you're a smart person, I'm sure, and have already figured out what the source of the slurping could have been.

The 'dillo had fallen for my trap. It was in the cage, going to town on the feast I'd laid out for it. I peered over the porch railing, adjusting my eyesight to the cage next to Tonya's garden. There was definitely some kind of activity going on there. Armadillo-sized activity. Its pink glow lit up the interior like a cotton candy factory. I finally understood why movie villains chuckled when their plans fell into place. There was simply no better feeling in the world.

"You fuckin' idiot," I taunted, and pulled the rope.

The gate came down perfectly, just as I had visualized.

Then the armadillo turned around and pushed the gate open with its head and casually exited the cage, which was the opposite of what I'd visualized.

Only then did it occur to me that the gate had a latch lock, and obviously wouldn't have enabled without someone physically sliding it into place after shutting it.

"Fuck," I whispered, watching in horror as the armadillo trotted through my yard with a full belly. It seemed to stumble a little bit with its movements, and I realized the little fucker was drunk. From *my* beer.

Without thinking, I raised the shotgun and fired. I don't know where the shot ended up but it was nowhere near my target. The back window of a neighbor's car did explode around the same time, but personally I believe that was unrelated. All my shotgun succeeded in doing was spooking the 'dillo into picking up its pace. It fled in chaotic hops, and I thought for sure it was going to disappear either in a hole or down the street, only to be proven wrong when it jumped directly into a fire hydrant in front of our house.

There was a loud *thunk* noise, and then the armadillo landed in the grass and rolled onto its back.

It stopped moving after that.

"Holy shit," I said, then cautiously left my porch and approached the motionless creature until I was standing

over it. The silly sumbitch had gone and killed itself, I thought, but no, its belly was moving ever so slightly—lifting up and down, up and down. Still breathing. Still alive. Which meant it'd simply knocked itself out, which somehow felt even more pathetic. I pointed my shotgun at it and considered splattering its entire existence next to the fire hydrant, but something about the situation just didn't sit right. This wasn't how things were supposed to go. There was no honor in this. A man didn't shoot something when it was unconscious. A man waited until it could fight back, until it could properly defend itself. I owed the armadillo that much, I reckoned. Or maybe I didn't owe it shit. Maybe I was simply a coward. It was possible both were equally true.

But I also couldn't leave it out here to wake up and get away from me again. That much I was certain of. So I reached down and grasped both of the armadillo's tails and scooped it up in the air. Its limp body swung back and forth, still out cold, like an extremely on-brand Texas pendulum. I tossed the sleeping beast into the cage, then latched the gate shut and brought the whole thing into the house, along with my shotgun and porch TV. I laid the cage in the center of the living room and sat down on the couch in front of it, shotgun over my lap, finger near the trigger—just in case—and promptly fell back asleep as the unconscious creature's pink glow bathed my skin. There was something about its smell, I thought, that made me feel calm. Like soaking in a hot bubble bath.

I would have probably slept until morning, too, if Officer Sebastian Dipshit didn't stop by less than thirty minutes later.

This time I was smart enough to stash my shotgun out of sight before opening the door. Even though I had plenty right to have one. Even though I had done nothing wrong. Even though he was a punk-ass wife-thieving cop. I didn't want there to be any interruptions or distractions now that I finally had trapped the 'dillo.

The cop was waiting on my porch, ghost-white, obviously scared like a little bitch about something.

"What do you want?" I asked.

"Oh, hi," he said, "it's, uh, it's me again."

"Tonya send you?"

He cocked his head, feigning puzzlement. "Uh, no, dispatch did."

"What the fuck did you just call my wife?" Suddenly I wished I hadn't stashed the shotgun, after all.

Trembling, the cop gestured to a radio device strapped to his shoulder. "We received another report of gunfire tonight."

"What does that have to do with me?"

"Um, well." The cop glanced over his shoulder, toward the house across the street. "Well, you see. Your neighbor over there? Someone shot up their car tonight, and, uh—"

"That could have been anybody."

"Right, sure, I get that, sir, but I was curious if you at least saw something?"

I laughed. "It don't matter one lick if I did or not. I ain't no snitch."

"Sir?"

I shook my head, already disgusted with this interaction. What the hell did Tonya see in this parasite? I stepped back to close the door, then the cop screamed and I froze in my tracks, followed his gaze behind me at the cage in the living room.

The 'dillo had woken from its stupor. Instead of panicking, or trying to bust loose from its new prison, it instead was busy slurping away at the beer-soaked dirt, both of its tails wagging like the happiest little animal that ever lived.

"What kind of dog is that?" the cop cried out, and I nearly slapped him across the face right then and there.

"That ain't no dog, you dumb shit," I told him. "That there is an armadillo."

He calmed. "Wow. I've never seen one up close like this before. I . . . I didn't know they glowed like that."

THE 'DILLO

He was talking to me like we were friendly, which further enraged me. "Go find your own 'dillo, this one's mine."

"What are you gonna do with it?"

"Never you mind that," I said. "All you need to do is go back to your luxurious condo or whatever the hell you live in and tell Tonya that it's all been taken care of, that there ain't gonna be nothin' else wreaking havoc in her garden no further. Tell her that her *husband* has once again saved the day."

The cop paused, taking in what I'd just said, then nodded and said, "Uh, okay."

There was something about the way he responded, though, that made me doubt he had any real intention of relaying the message.

Which was why, once Officer Pipsqueak drove away, I tried video-messaging her on my cell phone.

The first couple calls, she didn't answer. But that was okay. I was sure she was just sleeping and hadn't heard her phone yet. So I kept trying. In the meantime, I worked my way through a few more beers and splashed a little bit extra through the cage for the armadillo. It seemed grateful, the poor oblivious bastard. It had no idea that this would be its final meal. Few seldom do, though. Most people never realize they've done the last of something until it's too late, until they're breathing their final breaths and looking upon their past with a heavy, wet sigh of regret. And that's if they're lucky. A lot of folks don't even realize they're dying. One second they're going on about their day, worrying about trivial bullshit like bills and what gender M&Ms might be, then suddenly, just like that, they cease to be. The light switch's been flipped and that's that, mattress man. Maybe *they* were the lucky ones, come to think about it. The not-knowers.

It took a while, but Tonya eventually answered the phone. She was sitting on a couch in what appeared to be a living room. What a coincidence. I was doing the exact same thing.

She squinted into the camera. "Wayne? You got any idea what time it is?"

"Oh, I'm sorry, did I wake you?" I asked, reciting a line I'd rehearsed before making the call. Of course I knew it was late. She was an early sleeper. I figured there was zero chance she would have been awake when I called, which was why I kept doing it until she finally woke up. One of the most essential qualities of any romantic gesture was the element of surprise. Ask anyone.

"No, I wasn't asleep yet," she told me. "Sebastian and I were watching television."

Something in my brain short-circuited. "Television? At this hour? What the hell could you have been watching, woman?"

"*How to with John Wilson.*"

"How to do *what* with *who* now?"

"That's the name of the show," she explained. "*How to with John Wilson*. It's sophisticated."

"Well I ain't ever heard of no goddamn show called that."

"It's streaming on HBO Max."

I chortled smugly. "Don't you know anything, Tonya? It's called Just Max now. They rebranded."

Tonya paused, then glanced at someone offscreen and whispered, "Is that true?" A beat passed, then she shrugged and said to me, "I'm still learning about all of this." Another pause, then: "Question is, how do *you* know about it?"

"I know a lot of things about a lot of stuff, you'd be surprised," I said, wondering if I sounded as flirtatious as I intended. "Anyway, the reason I called you tonight is I thought you'd be interested in seeing something."

"Seeing what?" she asked, hesitation in her voice. "You're . . . you're not going to show me your pecker again, are you?"

I had no idea what she was talking about. "I told you I wouldn't," I said, then cleared my throat. "Now, are you ready for your surprise?"

Tonya rolled her eyes. "Only if you hurry. I don't know how long we're allowed to keep this show paused before Just Max double-charges us."

"Well, Tonya, you know, I took everything you told me under consideration. I mean it. I thought about it long and hard. And I get it. I haven't always backed you up. I haven't always been there for you. I recognize my failures perfectly well," I told her, and finished off my latest can of beer. "All of that is to say that you don't have to worry about the old me anymore. I'm a changed man. I take action now. I take care of business."

"What . . . what are you talking about?" she asked.

"What am I talking about? Baby, I'll show you what I'm talking about."

I reversed the camera on my phone, revealing the caged armadillo slurping boozed dirt.

She leaned closer to her own screen, squinting, then said, "Oh, you got a dog? What's that light you got strapped to it?"

I resisted the urge to fling my phone against the wall. "That ain't no dog, dammit! That's the 'dillo. You know. *The* 'dillo. The one you wanted me to take care. I got it, baby. I fucking got it."

"Oh," she said, then grimaced. "Why . . . why is it in the house?"

"I trapped it with beer and insects."

"But why?"

For some reason she still wasn't getting it. I redirected the camera to the shotgun next to me. "I thought maybe you'd like to witness its execution."

"Excuse me?"

"After everything it did to your garden, you know? Some good old-fashioned revenge."

"Wayne, do not shoot that thing."

I nodded along and said, "Yeah, I know, not in the living room where there's carpet. I ain't a moron, you know. I was planning on doing it in the bathtub. Easy cleanup."

"Wayne, do not shoot it *anywhere*."

"What are you talking about?" I said. "You got some other idea how I'm supposed to end its life?"

There was a loud sigh on the other end of the call. "I already told you, Wayne, none of this between you and me has anything to do with armadillos. It is far more complicated than that."

"Wait a second," I said, something just then occurring to me. "Who's there with you?"

"What are you talking about?"

"There's a man there. You said so yourself."

"It's Sebastian. I told you about him already."

"Bullshit," I said, and stood up from the couch, started pacing around the living room. "Your lover boy just left my house not that long ago. I know he's working tonight. Jesus Christ, woman, how many men do you got at this point?" I asked this question with excitement in my voice. I was thrilled to learn that she was cheating on that cuck of a police officer with someone else. I was then immediately crushed to realize that this meant she was also further away from ever returning to our marriage. If anything, this concreted the fact that she had no intention of ever moving back in with me. I was old news. I was spoiled garbage. I was the past.

I collapsed on the couch and stared at the armadillo. It had stopped slurping beer dirt and was now facing me. Somehow it looked just as depressed as I felt.

"Please don't call me again," Tonya said, and hung up the phone. I studied the blank screen on my own device and thought, oh, that must be why they call that one show *Black Mirror*, and tossed it on the empty cushion next me. Not that I'd ever seen *Black Mirror*, of course. But I'd seen plenty of folks discussing it on Facebook to be aware of its general existence as a piece of pop culture. *How to with John Wilson*, on the other hand, I had no fucking idea if that was even real or if Tonya had made it up to distract from her latest act of adultery. Perhaps the fella she was

shacking up with tonight had been named John Wilson. If that was the case, I did not want to find out what, exactly, he was showing my wife how to do.

The armadillo was still staring at me. It looked sympathetic. Like it understood I'd just realized my marriage was beyond repair. I considered whether or not I still wanted to execute this thing. What would I gain out of dragging it to my bathtub, pressing the barrel of my shotgun against its little rodent face, and pulling the trigger? Would that honestly make me feel better? Murder wasn't going to bring Tonya back. It was quite possible nothing would at this point. I fantasized what my house would be like completely alone. At least with this 'dillo here I could have some kind of company. Something I could talk to besides myself and inanimate objects. Could these creatures live in houses with humans, though? Would it be satisfied here, or would it long for the great outdoors, the safety of a never-ending hole in the ground? I could bring more dirt inside. More bugs. More beer. Anything it needed. Why not? Who was there to stop me?

No one. There was no one.

I unlatched the cage and lifted the gate, then kneeled at the opening and waited for the 'dillo to approach. I made no sudden movements. I did not force it to come to me. I held out my hand when it was close enough and said, "I've decided not to kill you, after all."

As a thank you, the creature licked my fingers.

I scooped it out of the cage and plopped back down on the couch, cradling it in my lap. If the creature smelled calming, then actual physical touch was that sensation multiplied by a hundred. Little fucker was like a stress ball or something, I don't know what. But the more I caressed its pink glowing shell, the more relaxed I felt. In fact, I couldn't remember ever feeling this good in my whole stupid life. I cranked the volume on the television and, together, we watched late-night reruns of sitcoms from the 1990s until I fell asleep.

In the morning, the 'dillo was gone. I studied the emptiness in my lap and thought, well, I have done been truly abandoned. I thought, cancel culture strikes again. I thought, I will die alone. I thought, aw shucks.

But then I heard a rustling in the kitchen, and upon investigating the noise discovered the 'dillo had not ditched me after all. Something in my heart fluttered and warmed. There the critter was next to a knocked-over trash can, digging its way through moldy fast food wrappers and empty beer cans. I wasn't sure I'd taken the garbage out since Tonya left me. The kitchen had a certain odor that I hadn't noticed until now. She would have never approved. Personally, I sorta liked the smell. Made me feel masculine in a way I seldom got the chance to experience.

The 'dillo seemed to be paying extra attention to the cans. Sticking its little tongue through the mouth holes, trying to salvage any remaining drops I might have missed before discarding. "Aww," I said, "you're just a thirsty little fella, ain't you?" Then I paused, thinking things over. "Wait, *are* you a fella?" I realized I had no idea. Did armadillos have genitalia? This was new territory for me. I picked the armadillo up from the trash and said, "I apologize if this embarrasses you," and flipped it over, hands clasped around either side of its pink protective shell.

Or, I guess, *his* pink protective shell. I spotted a small armadillo pecker, but no testicles.

Maybe armadillos didn't have testicles. I knew dogs did. Bulls, too. What about cats? I could not imagine a cat with testicles. The image did not compute in my brain. Mice? No fucking way. Mice definitely did not have testicles. Suddenly I couldn't stop imagining a mouse with a giant dick, just dragging it across rough surfaces as he scurried away from enemies. I pictured a mouse getting

only his penis stuck in a trap and I almost started crying. I decided to stop thinking about that. Elephants probably had them. Wasn't there a whole disease named after elephants concerning grotesquely large balls?

But I'd never heard anything about armadillos. Of course, it wasn't like I'd ever put any real research into the topic. Until that morning, the thought had never even crossed my mind. I suddenly felt mighty uncomfortable spending so much time focusing on my new friend's genitals. If he spoke like a human, I would have just asked him, but as far as I could tell the only language he could speak was some form of anxious chittering.

Before setting him back down, I took a moment to study the rest of his underside. The 'dillo's belly was surprisingly soft and furry, nothing like the armor encompassing his back. I gave it a little rub, and he stuck out his tongue, which was thin and long, almost reptilian. "You like that, don't you?" I said, giggling, and rubbed him. "Oh, you little freak, you love it."

He chittered in response. Less anxious-sounding this time. It sounded more like he was content with his place in the world.

"How about some breakfast, little buddy?" I asked, and I swear to god he nodded his little head. I got us each a beer and returned to the living room. His I poured into the dirt mound occupying his cage. Mine I drank straight from the can. I didn't need dirt like he did. I wasn't an armadillo.

Together we had our breakfast and watched early-morning judge shows on television. Afterward, I locked him back in the cage and draped a blanket over the top, then locked up and went to work.

"I'll be back soon," I assured him as I walked out the door. "I promise."

At my job, I could barely think about anything besides the 'dillo. And sure, I guess it's true this creature had plagued my thoughts for many days now, but this time it was different. Now, when I thought about the animal, I did not imagine his guts spattered across my front lawn. Instead I fantasized about petting his belly. I smiled at the idea of him waiting for me to get home so we could drink beer and watch wrestling together. How funny, I thought, how quickly something like this could flipflop. Less than twenty-four hours ago I had desperately yearned to be the armadillo's executioner. Now he was my only friend in the world. He was all I cared about.

My job, my stupid job. It was a meaningless job. A job that never excited me. I had coworkers, sure, and sometimes we shot the shit, but I found I could no longer relate to them like I might've been able to once upon a time ago. Many of them were still in healthy marriages. None of them had an armadillo in their house. Dogs, sure. Maybe a couple cats. Even a snake or two. But I was the only one with an armadillo. I was certain of it.

There's no point in describing my job. What I had to do to pay the bills. Imagine something boring, and exhausting. Something that made me sweat a lot and get dirty. Something that required a lot of heavy lifting. Most of us brought thermoses of soup for lunch, or sandwiches in ziploc bags. I was never prepared like that. Instead I drove to a nearby Valero gas station and purchased a footlong meatball or BLT from the Subway built inside it. This was my routine. It wasn't exciting, but it was mine.

Usually, I ate in my truck and watched YouTube on my phone. Today I'd found a couple clips about armadillos I was eager to deep-dive into. Maybe I could learn something educational about my new pal. But before I press PLAY on the first video, the screen burst with activity as I received a call from Tonya. At first I thought maybe I was hallucinating that she was calling me. After all, hadn't she made things extremely clear last night where things stood?

THE 'DILLO

With a trembling hand, I laid down my footlong meatball sandwich and answered the phone.

"He-hello?" I said, and through the Bluetooth speakers in my truck, Tonya replied.

"Wayne, is that you?"

"The one and only," I said, and wondered if I sounded as cool as I did in my head.

"I just wanted to check in after last night, and make sure you hadn't . . . uh, you know."

"Killed the 'dillo?"

"Oh, god, did you?"

"No, ma'am. The 'dillo and I are tight now."

"You're tight?"

"That's right. I'm keeping him."

"Wayne, you can't keep an armadillo."

Rage heated my cheeks. "What gives you any right to say what I can and can't keep? I thought you moved out."

"I'm just saying—you know they're bad for you, right? Like, they carry leprosy and shit. You're gonna get sick."

"They carry *what*?" I said. "Woman, what the hell are you talking about?"

"Leprosy, Wayne. It's like a disease or something."

"What kind of disease?" I had no idea what the hell she was talking about.

"Like a fuckin' zombie disease, Wayne. I don't know the specifics. I'm not a doctor."

I started cracking up. I couldn't believe it took me this long to realize my wife was batshit crazy. "Wait, do you think zombies are real?" I said. "And you think they happen because of armadillos? What the hell have these new boyfriends of yours been giving you?"

Please don't say good dick, I immediately started praying, *please don't say good dick.*

My prayers were answered. She didn't address that last question whatsoever. Instead, she said, "You didn't touch it with your bare hands, did you?"

"What business is that of yours, exactly?" I said. "I

thought you weren't my wife no more." I almost added, *Or have you experienced a change of heart?* but managed to bite my tongue at the last second. I didn't want her to know that I'd still be open to reconciliation. I'd already tried that and look at how she'd ended up treating me. I wasn't going to fall for that again. No, sir.

"Well, shit, Wayne—just because I don't want to live together no more don't mean I don't care about you still. I'm concerned, goddammit!"

"Oh, yeah?" I said, feeling like I was about to explode. "Well I don't need your concern! Save it for Sebastian and his pathetic little badge. Me and my 'dillo will be plenty fine without you, devil woman!"

I hung up before she could respond and smirked at myself in the rearview mirror, thinking, that'll teach her. Thinking, this will win her back. Thinking, oh god what have I done.

I finished my Subway sandwich and returned to work.

After my shift, I stopped at my uncle's bait and tackle shop. It was as if he hadn't budged an inch since the day before. Even the same train crash compilation boomed out of his laptop.

"Uncle! Are you alive?" I shouted from across the store, terrified he might've fallen victim to a heart attack or brain aneurysm shortly after yesterday's conversation.

He glanced my way and smiled. "Am I alive?" He thought about the question far longer than any other person would've spent. "Well, I reckon that depends on your definition of alive, Nephew. Am I still a functioning component of a computer simulating what we perceive to be life? I can answer, safely, yes. Any deeper answer would require far more consideration than I am sober enough to give."

"I thought you'd stopped smoking weed."

"True," my uncle said, "but I never said anything about giving up DMT."

I didn't know enough about DMT to know whether or not I should be concerned about him. Either way, he seemed like he was living his best life. He had his bait and tackle shop. He had his train crashing compilation videos. He had his DMT. He had it made, far as I could tell.

"What brings you around again so soon? You miss your dear uncle's company?"

"I need another bucket."

"Another bucket?" he said, practically shouting over the laptop's volume. "Another bucket of *what*? Of dirt? Of insects?"

"Yes, sir."

"'Yes, sir' to which one?"

"Well, I reckon to both. In fact, let's make it two buckets this time."

"Jesus Christ Almighty, Wayne, you fixin' to wipe out every goddamn armadillo in the great state of Texas?"

I shook my head, impatient. "Nah, there's been a change of plans. I ain't trying to kill him anymore. We're pals now."

"Pals? The hell you mean—pals?"

"I mean exactly what I said."

He crossed his arms over his chest, determined to hear a better explanation. "Now how the hell does a fella—a grown man—get to become pals with an armadillo of all things?"

"How does a fella become pals with a dog? How does a fella become pals with *anything*?" I said. "We bonded. We shared a moment. We got drunk together and we watched TV."

My uncle hesitated. "You're saying this 'dillo drinks beer?"

"That's what I'm saying."

"*And* watches TV?"

"Yessir."

"What does it like to watch?"

"He seems pretty partial to professional wrestling."

"It drinks beer and watches professional wrestling. Holy jumping Jesus." My uncle smirked. "Now that's a pretty goddamn cool armadillo right there."

An idea struck me. "You wanna come meet him?"

My uncle gave the idea some consideration. "You know, I don't really get out much these days. Someone's gotta run the shop, after all."

"Shit, Uncle, don't you ever close?"

"Does Amazon close? Of course not. Every second I'm not open, I lose a potential customer to some soul-less robot."

"I don't think Amazon sells buckets of live insects," I told him.

"Amazon *is* a bucket of live insects," my uncle said, and spit something in a nearby trash can.

"You coming over or not?"

"That depends," he said. "You got any beer?"

I didn't, but I was planning on stopping for more on the way home, anyway, which was all he needed to hear. We collected two more buckets of dirt and bugs and drove to the closest H-E-B. My uncle waited in the truck as I went inside for the drinks. I'd asked him why he didn't just follow me in his own car, and he told me his license had recently been suspended for reasons he refused to get into, other than hinting that the incident might've also resulted in his name getting added to some sort of government terrorist watch list. Most of the time, when it came to my uncle, it was smarter not to probe for more information. This felt like one of those times.

Beer acquired, we booked it back home. My uncle asked if I'd stop and pick up some Burger Boy along the way, but got real quiet when I asked who he expected to pay for it. I told him I had some old corn dogs in the freezer. We could have ourselves a regular-ol' corn dog party, just like the old days. He didn't seem that excited about the idea but also I didn't hear him offering to foot

the bill for Burger Boy, so I didn't feel too bad about it, truth be told. Wasn't a goddamn thing wrong with corn dogs. Personally I never felt more like a patriotic American than when I was dunking a couple breaded wieners in a puddle of yellow mustard. They didn't do that kind of shit in other countries. I would have heard about it by now, trust me.

At the front door, before even opening it, I could hear the 'dillo inside playing with one of the squeaky toys I'd purchased. I froze there with the key halfway inserted in the lock. A smile warmed my face. The sense of accomplishment overwhelmed me. I had done something right. Keeping this animal, not killing him, this had been the right decision. For once in my life I hadn't fucked everything up. It felt good to admit this to myself. It felt incredible.

"Poor little guy," I said, eager to get through the door, "I bet he's hungry."

When we got inside, everything was where I'd left it, and why wouldn't it be? What else were you expecting? For the armadillo to have escaped his cage and destroyed my living quarters? Ripped my pillows open, maybe, or smeared his feces all over the walls? Well this wasn't no kids' movie, and the 'dillo wasn't no St. Bernard Beethoven dog. He was still where I'd confined him, perfectly at peace with the world as he gnawed on the rubber chicken. I held out my hand toward him, gesturing for my uncle to take the sight in, and my uncle gasped right there in the doorway, dropping both buckets of dirt. Luckily they landed right-side-up without spilling anything on the carpet.

"Jesus Christ," he said, "what the fuck is that?"

"The hell you mean?" I said, already regretting dragging him home with me. "That's the 'dillo."

My uncle stared at me like I was playing some kind of practical joke on him. He said nothing more, so I shut the door behind him and headed into the kitchen to refrigerate

the new beer, then I pulled open my freezer door and started scavenging for dinner.

"Say, how many corn dogs you want, anyway? Two, or what?"

Then I realized he hadn't followed me into the kitchen, but was still in the living room. I peeked around the corner and caught him kneeling next to the cage. He looked terrified.

"What the hell's your problem?" I asked him.

"Nephew," he said, not taking his eyes off the 'dillo, "where . . . where did you get this thing?"

"I already told you." I nodded toward the picture window. "Right out there, in the front yard."

"Was this the first time you'd ever seen it?"

I shook my head, irritated and on the verge of kicking him out of my house. "Nah, man, remember I told you he'd been coming around for weeks now, fucking up Tonya's garden and shit."

"And this is the same one?" he asked. "From all those other times, I mean."

"Well, yeah, of course. Why are you acting like such a weirdo?" I opened the gate and picked up the 'dillo, holding him against my chest like a little baby. My uncle gasped and stepped back, trembling. "You think he's gonna hurt you or something? Relax. What did I tell you? He's cool. He drinks beer. He watches professional wrestling. There ain't nothing to worry about, man."

The 'dillo stretched in my arms and gave my face a little lick. Nothing in this world had ever loved me in such a way. I hugged him tighter, but not too tight to hurt him or suffocate him or anything like that, just tight enough to show that the feeling was mutual. And yeah, I wasn't no fool, I was able to recognize that perhaps my adoration for this pest had developed at an alarming speed, but when had love ever taken its time? After a brief moment of consideration, I kissed the top of his head, too. My uncle, having witnessed this act of intimacy, made a sound like he was going to vomit.

"Oh, would you quit being such a pussy?" I said. "You would kiss a dog, wouldn't you? A little kitty cat? Practically zero difference. Only this fella has a shell. And you know what? That don't make him any less adorable. In fact, I'd wager that it adds to his charm." As an act of defiance, I raised the armadillo to my face and gave his pink glowing armored shell a long, exaggerated lick. I mentally prepared for it to taste awful and was thrown off guard to experience the complete opposite sensation.

All feeling in my hands numbed, and the 'dillo dropped to the floor, landing on his feet and scurrying away. My uncle yelped and leapt onto the couch despite the fact that the 'dillo's target seemed to be somewhere in the kitchen. I thought about following him to see what he was up to. I thought real hard. Unfortunately that was all I could do. My legs refused to move. They were paralyzed, stuck in place. Like my limbs had been dipped in drying cement. *What the heck is this all about,* I tried to say, but my lips also could not move. Yet I did not regret licking the armadillo, because the taste currently exploding in my taste buds was unlike anything I'd ever felt in my life. I didn't know how to describe it then, and I sure as hell don't know how to describe it now. Imagine an orgasm, but inside your mouth. Now, I don't mean taking a load of jism between the lips. Don't misinterpret my words, dammit. I mean imagine your mouth is the source of the orgasm. A tongue that's been swapped with someone's clitoris. I don't know whose. Anybody's, I suppose. It doesn't matter. But can you imagine that? It's okay if you can't. This isn't your story. This isn't your life. You don't need to do anything but listen. What I'm trying to say is it was *overwhelming,* okay, but in a good way. In a way that made my body shut down for a moment, unable to comprehend anything further.

And then I lost the ability to continue standing. My legs transformed into rubber. My body crumpled. Somehow I landed in a sitting position on the couch behind me. The

back of my skull bounced off the wall, but if it was painful I didn't feel anything. I didn't feel a thing besides a heavy intoxication of pure bliss. I'd only taken morphine once in my life, several years back when I fucked my leg up in a car accident, and the hospital introduced a drip to my veins. All of the pain in my body and all of the sorrow in my soul dissipated, and suddenly it was as if I existed not *on* a cloud but *as* a cloud. That was how I felt tonight, after licking the 'dillo's shell. It had turned me into a cloud.

"I'm a goddamn cloud!" somebody yelled. Only later would I conclude that the exclamation had originated from my own lungs.

"You're a what?" my uncle asked a few seconds later, or maybe a few hours later. Time was hard to interpret by then. He was still standing on the couch, towering over me scared shitless. Slowly he got down, never looking away from the kitchen entrance where the armadillo had disappeared. If he was making noise in there, I couldn't hear him. Already sound had started meaning something different to me. I wasn't processing it like normal folks did. Everything sounded delayed, far away, muffled, distorted. Like being under water, but in a pleasant way.

I know my uncle kept asking me if I was okay, if he should call an ambulance, if he should call Tonya, but I couldn't figure out how to respond to any of his questions. I think I was drooling a lot and maybe grinning sorta stupidly. If I had better control over my vocals, I would have encouraged my uncle to go have himself a lick upon the 'dillo's majestic armor so we could share this beautiful moment together.

Then my uncle leaned real close to my ear and whispered, "Wayne, I don't think that thing is an armadillo."

"Hogwash," I tried to say, but my tongue refused to

participate and what I ended up saying sounded incomprehensible. A small spike of anger penetrated my high. What would cause my uncle to start telling such horrible lies? Why was he trying to sabotage my new friendship? I reckoned he was jealous, most likely. He certainly didn't have any friends. He spent every day at his bait and tackle shop, alone. Maybe he thought this armadillo would corrupt our own relationship and I'd stop checking in on him from time to time. Which was a ridiculous fear. I would never abandon my uncle. We were family. Flesh and blood.

"Are you trying to tell me you've ever seen an armadillo that looks like . . . like that one?" He gestured toward the kitchen. "I mean, Jesus Christ, Wayne, I ain't ever seen nothing that looks like that thing."

If I could have talked, I would have asked him if he'd ever actually seen a live armadillo up close before. Not counting road kill. Not counting videos on YouTube. But a real, in-your-face 'dillo. Because I sure as hell hadn't, and I was willing to bet neither had he. Which was why the one in my house appeared so unnatural to him. He'd never seen anything quite like one. That didn't mean he wasn't a real armadillo, though. It just meant my uncle was uneducated, and it was my responsibility to teach him a proper lesson, seeing as this was my house and all.

"Okay, I'll show you," I slurred, and after an intense moment of concentration somehow managed to stand back up again. "Just . . . just wait here, goddamn you."

I left my uncle next to the couch and stumbled into the kitchen, expecting to find the trash can knocked over again but this time the armadillo was simply standing against the refrigerator door, frantically clawing at its smooth texture. He must've been able to detect the beer I'd stashed inside it.

"Oh, you thirsty, little fella?" I said, then had to pause and lean against the table as the whole room started spinning. The armadillo stopped scratching the fridge and

turned around so he could study me with his peculiar rodent-like eyes. "Boy, I'll tell you what, kiddo, whatever was on your shell sure has me feeling all sorts of strange tonight."

The 'dillo made a chipper chittering noise, as if he understood perfectly what I was saying. And why couldn't that be true? Why couldn't an armadillo understand a man? And why couldn't a man understand an armadillo? Who makes up these rules? Who says someone can't do something? He understood me, and I understood him, and what I understood was he desperately wanted a beer, and you know what? So did I.

I recovered from my brief vertigo and fetched three cans from the fridge, figuring my uncle would want one to calm his nerves a bit. Truth be told, his behavior was embarrassing me tonight. I never would have shown him the armadillo if I'd known he planned on acting like a total bitch. I set his can down on the table and popped open the tabs on the remaining two. I took a deep chug from my beer and then felt bad that I was drinking without the 'dillo, so I got down a bowl from the cupboard and poured the other opened can into it. Together we drank in silence. Somewhere in the living room, my uncle called my name. He asked if I was okay. I screamed back, "I have never been better in my whole goddamn life, uncle!" Our beers were finished. I popped open the tab from the can I was saving for my uncle and poured half of it into the armadillo's bowl, then I chugged the rest. I belched. The armadillo glanced up at me and belched, too.

"I didn't know armadillos could belch," I said, and then I thought the 'dillo probably didn't know humans could belch, either, and the longer we were friends I imagined the more we would continue to surprise each other about our individual species. What else would we have in common? This prospect greatly excited me. I could not wait to discover more thrilling similarities. I picked up the creature and said, "Do you mind if I do it again?" And, in

case he didn't understand exactly what I was referring to, I clarified: "I mean, do you mind if I lick your shell again? Like I did earlier?" The armadillo didn't make any movement or noise indicating he preferred I keep my tongue to myself. I chose to take his lack of reaction as enough consent—after all, this was still an armadillo we were dealing with here—and I gave his shell another caress with my tongue. This time I didn't rush through the process. I started at one end of the armor and dragged my tongue clear across to the other side.

Afraid of losing control of my limbs again and accidentally busting my head open on the tiled kitchen floor, I scrambled for a seat at the table, still holding the 'dillo out in front of me with both hands like someone might present a holy artifact. And, in that moment and every moment afterward, that's exactly what he was to me: a holy artifact, which I would protect at all costs.

Every color in the kitchen intensified. My pupils could barely comprehend everything transforming before me. Slowly I laid the 'dillo on the table. If I held him any longer, I would have only ended up dropping him again. He tiptoed over to me and kissed my chin. I wondered if he experienced anything similar to what I was going through after licking him. Somehow I doubted it. Tonya had licked my face thousands of times and she never once got high from it, as far as I could recall. My flesh was boring. It was ordinary. I was no armadillo. I was nothing.

So why kiss me then, right? If he wasn't benefiting from it the way I was benefiting. Why does anybody kiss anybody, then? To express their love. To say, *Hey, I care about you*. He was clearly grateful I'd taken him in under my roof and bought him lots of fun toys to play with, not to mention the beer and buckets of dirt and bugs. Most armadillos, I imagined, were never lucky enough to have someone like me in their lives—and, you know what? Most humans were never lucky enough to have a 'dillo like this fella in their lives. He was grateful for me and I was grateful

for him. Most relationships—purely platonic or otherwise—it's important to frequently acknowledge how fortunate they make you feel. Otherwise you might forget. Look at what happened with Tonya. I'm not saying I did anything wrong there. I'm saying *she* forgot. She took for granted the life we once had together. Hypnotized by a pig with fancy gadgets. I thought I wanted her back but now, sitting in this kitchen with the 'dillo's magical spine fluids upon my tongue, I experienced a new kind of clarity. Not only was I not sure if I could ever forgive her for this treachery, I was no longer sure if I *wanted* to forgive her, either. Maybe this separation was a blessing in disguise. After all, without her absence in my life, would I have ever welcomed the armadillo into my home? Would we have ever become best friends?

Without giving it too much thought, I spun my new pal around atop the table and suctioned my lips around his armored shell. This time, instead of licking, I chose to slurp the moist layer generating through his rough texture. If licking the 'dillo had been akin to chugging a beer, then slurping him like this was more along the lines of taking ten consecutive shots of hard liquor. When I said, "Holy motherfucking shit," afterward, I meant it with all my heart.

I felt my body sinking against the chair. Somehow I managed not to tip out of it.

Everything was blissfully heavy.

Across the kitchen, next to the living room entryway, I spotted my uncle running toward me. Except, despite being in a classic runner's pose, the man wasn't actually moving. He wasn't blinking. He wasn't doing a goddamn thing.

"Uncle," I whispered, "are you frozen?"

He did not respond, which in its own way was enough of an answer.

I glanced at the 'dillo for confirmation. "Is he frozen?"

And the 'dillo nodded his little head, and said, "In a way, yes. More accurately, it's you and I who have

dramatically sped up. Your uncle is still moving at a normal speed. He is on his way to stop you from touching me. He plans to kill me. Most likely with the bottom of his boot."

"Oh," I said, then added, "Hey, I didn't know armadillos could talk."

"Everything talks," the 'dillo said. "But not everything has something to say."

His voice sounded like poetic TV static. I don't know if that makes sense. If you're having trouble hearing it, that's okay. Just imagine a famous celebrity's voice instead if that's easier. Someone like Sinbad or Pauly Shore perhaps. It doesn't matter too much to me since I know what he really sounded like and nothing you imagine will ever change that.

"How are we sped up?" I asked.

"It's just something I can do," the 'dillo said. "And now you can do it with me, since we've officially bonded."

"Because I licked you?"

"Because you licked me."

"Was that okay for me to do? It wasn't weird, right?"

The 'dillo considered the question, then said, "It was definitely pretty weird, but it was also okay. I didn't know what would happen but I was eager to find out. If anyone was going to do it, I'm glad it was you. No human has ever shared their beer with me before. You're something special, Wayne."

"Do you have a name?"

"Of course I have a name. You think I don't have a name?"

"No, it's just . . . you haven't told me yet. I don't know what to call you. I've just been saying the 'dillo."

He took a step back on the table. "You've been calling me a dildo? Wayne, I thought we were tight."

"No, not dildo. 'Dillo. Like, armadillo."

"Oh." He paused, clearly uncomfortable. "Well, I think that sucks. Don't ever call me that again."

"Shit, man, I'm sorry." Tears started welling at my eyes. "What's your name, then? I'll never call you a 'dillo again."

"Eugene."

"Eugene?"

"Yeah, my name is Eugene. You have a problem with that, or something?" The 'dillo—I mean, *Eugene*—seemed overly defensive about his name. I hoped I hadn't offended him.

"No, man. Eugene is a cool name. I just wanted to make sure I had it right. Shit, I wish *my* name was Eugene. You think I like *Wayne*? I fucking *hate* Wayne." I peeked back over at my uncle. I was no expert at perception, but I was pretty sure he had moved a couple inches forward since the beginning of our conversation. "Hey, can he hear us talking right now?"

Eugene shook his head. "No, not at the speed we're traveling. We could recite entire Shakespeare plays before he managed to progress another foot. He wouldn't even perceive our lips moving, not that I have lips. I am, after all, a perfectly ordinary armadillo."

"Looks like you got lips to me, man."

"Oh." Eugene belched. His breath reeked of beer. "Then maybe armadillos have lips, after all."

"Well, I don't know dick about Shakespeare, if that's what you were planning on suggesting."

"No, not that . . . " Eugene cleared his little armadillo throat. "But, you know, there *is* something we do need to address."

"Other than the fact that you've fucked with time and also that you're talking to me?"

"I already told you, Wayne, this is all standard armadillo stuff."

"I know. I'm sorry. It's just a lot to take in."

"I understand that, but you need to listen to me now, okay? Because, yes, I've manipulated time a bit, but not

forever, and also this process isn't exactly . . . painless on my part, you know what I mean? Creating this privacy bubble for us to converse in, it's already starting to wipe me out. You ever try carrying a mattress by yourself, maybe up several flights of stairs? Not that I have, of course, seeing as I am an armadillo, but you get my point. You *do* get my point—right, Wayne?"

"Um, yeah," I lied, "definitely."

"Now, the reason I isolated us here in our own little pocket is something very bad is about to happen. As you can already see, your uncle is currently charging us. He has every intention of destroying me. He will smash me and stomp on my body and not stop until everything inside of me is splattered across the kitchen floor. He is doing this for two reasons. One, as you were saying earlier, he is extremely jealous of our friendship. He does not have many other people in his life, and he is terrified my presence will replace him and you'll stop checking in on him at his bait and tackle shop."

"Wait a second," I said. "I never said that out loud. I was only thinking it."

"Oh?" Eugene made a nervous chitter. "No, you're misremembering. You were monologuing for everybody to hear. Maybe you only thought you were thinking it."

"Well, I suppose that makes sense," I said, even if I still wasn't so sure.

"You do that a lot, you know. Narrating your thoughts when you're alone. Except you're not alone anymore. I'm here, and I'm never leaving you. I'm not like your wife. I'm here to stay." Before I could respond, he continued: "Now, the second reason your uncle is charging us is he is not actually your uncle—at least, not anymore. Your real uncle, the man who served as your ordained minister, is back at the bait and tackle shop. The only bit of him that you actually brought home tonight is his face, which—as you can see—is cleverly being worn like a mask upon his murderer and imposter."

"Wait, hold up there now. What are you trying to say?"

The 'dillo sighed, then gestured his two tails at the man in my kitchen. "That is not your uncle. He may look like your uncle, but trust me, your uncle is dead. He was killed. Tonight, if I had to guess."

"But . . . why? Who is this? What the hell are you talking about? I thought we were gonna drink beer and eat corn dogs tonight." I wanted to get up and pace around, but Eugene's weird time magic had me glued to the seat.

"Trust me, Wayne. I'm an armadillo. Of course I would have loved to only drink beer and eat corn dogs with you and your uncle. It's what armadillos like doing best. But, unfortunately, that isn't the reality we find ourselves in now. Because some fucking demon decided tonight of all nights to remove your uncle's face and wear it to trick you."

"Demon?" I squinted at my uncle. He didn't look like no demon. "What makes you so sure about this?"

"You think this is my first encounter with a demon? Demons hate armadillos. They hunt us constantly, because they know we can see through their disguises. It's one of our many special talents."

"Like being able to fuck with time."

" . . . Yes, just like that."

"So you're saying this demon killed my uncle? But why? For what reason?"

"I thought that would have been obvious, Wayne. To get closer to me. To catch me off my guard, so he can capture and torture me into telling him very confidential armadillo secrets, and then slowly end my life. Then, if I had to guess, kill you too. Probably even Tonya, come to think about it. Any loose ends. These demons, they're nothing if not thorough."

"I'm sorry, but this don't make a lick of sense."

"Is it any less unbelievable than a talking armadillo, Wayne?"

The little dude had a point. "Okay," I said. "Even if this is true, what are we supposed to do about it?"

Eugene let out a sigh of relief. "Finally, a reasonable question. What we're going to do is we're going to stop him, which I'll need your help doing, of course. After all, I do not have any thumbs, and—tell me if I'm mistaken here—but I believe it is much easier to hold a knife with a thumb."

"Knife? What knife?"

"The one over there, by the sink. You're going to stand up and get it, then come back over here and defend us."

Suddenly I no longer felt high in a good way. "I ain't gonna stab my uncle. I don't care even if he *is* a demon. I've gone this long without stabbing anybody and I'm not gonna break my streak now."

"I'm sorry, but when you invited me to move in with you, I was under the impression that you weren't a total pussy."

I could have cried. In fact, I *was* crying. "That ain't a nice thing to say to someone, you know. That ain't a nice thing to say at all."

"Would you relax, Wayne? Nobody is telling you to stab anybody. I am merely encouraging you to use the knife as a scare tactic. If he sees it, he'll stop trying to attack us. He'll pause and try to convince you to step aside so he can proceed with his plans of killing me. We can use that extra time to talk to him and get him to leave without any of us resorting to violence. Isn't that what you'd prefer, anyway?"

Eugene was correct. I did prefer that outcome over having to stab somebody. "How sure are you he's a demon?"

"Wayne. My brother in Christ. I am telling you, that guy is a fucking demon."

"Well this sucks," I said. "How am I supposed to get a knife, anyhow? I can hardly move."

"Oh? How about now?" Eugene made another weird chittering noise, and I found that I'd regained control of my body again.

"How about that," I said.

"Now get the knife, Wayne. Get it while I can still hold him back."

I won't lie. In that moment, I was a little spooked. For one thing, I was still trying to come to grips with the fact that armadillos could talk all this time. But also, could it have been true, what Eugene was saying? Was my uncle really dead? I never knew anybody who got murdered before. I sure as shit never knew anybody who got their face ripped off and worn by someone else like a mask. I'm sure you can't blame me if I was having trouble letting the news sink in. I'd like to see how anybody else would've handled the situation.

So yeah. I got up. I retrieved the knife Eugene was talking about. It was a big-ass one, too. A fella could split open a melon with a knife of this caliber. One whack was all it would've taken. I returned to the table, but I didn't sit down. Eugene told me not to. He said I had to stand in front of him, block him like a shield. He told me I oughta hold the knife out, too, so there was no mistaking it for anything but what it was. The demon had to know we meant business, otherwise there would be no reasoning with him.

This made sense to me then. Honestly, it makes sense to me now. Say what you will about 'dillos, but you couldn't claim they weren't a logical breed. I did as I was told. I held out the knife, tip first. Then I waited for something to happen.

"Okay, now what?" I asked, feeling foolish. When Eugene didn't answer right away, I glanced over my shoulder at the table and spotted him licking the rim clean from the last can of beer I'd left there.

He realized I was waiting on him, and backed away from the can. "Sorry, sorry. I guess I was still a little thirsty."

"It's all good, brother," I said, and I wondered if this was the first time a man had ever called an armadillo

brother. I hoped it was. There were very few other accomplishments in my past I could have been considered the first to do, but maybe this was one of them. I liked the sound of it.

"Okie dokie," Eugene said. "You ready?"

And before I could answer one way or the other, he made another chittering noise, then the whole room got unbearably loud, like how it sounds when a jet engine's about to take off. I tightened my grip on the knife handle, terrified this possible demon might slap it out of my hands the moment he saw it, but turns out that wasn't something I needed to worry about. When Eugene first fucked around with time, my uncle-demon must've been charging us at an awfully fast pace, because barely half a second passed after everything returned to normal before he ran directly into the knife.

Unfortunately, my uncle was much shorter than I am, making the blade the perfect height to puncture straight through his throat.

Which is exactly what happened.

I remained standing there for a moment, still holding the knife, trying to ascertain where the rest of my knife had disappeared, not quite believing that it was currently inside the neck of the man I'd once considered my uncle. Though Eugene had told me the truth, that this wasn't my uncle— except for the face— then the demon who'd killed him sure had been the exact height as my uncle, the exact goddamn build, and I'm sorry but that was one hell of a coincidence, if you ask me.

I let go of the knife.

My uncle-demon collapsed to the floor. Normal, American blood began pooling around his neck. The knife remained sticking out of him.

"Oh my god," I whispered, and sat back at the table. I

couldn't stop staring at the body. Couldn't stop thinking about how quickly he'd gone limp, how easy it'd been to take his life.

I kept trying to tell myself that this wasn't my uncle, that this was just some armadillo-hating demon, but I didn't have the same powers as Eugene. To me, this just looked like my uncle. My family. And I'd killed him. Stabbed him in the throat with a goddamn knife. The same knife Tonya used to use when cutting up fruits and vegetables. The very same. Holy fuck. What had I done?

"What have I done?" I repeated, this time out loud, and the 'dillo was more-than-pleased to answer.

"What you've done, Wayne, is slay yourself a juicy little demon. Pat yourself on the back for a job well done"

Pat myself on the back? I couldn't fathom the thought. I didn't feel like celebrating. I wanted to throw myself into a lake.

"Think about it this way, Wayne," Eugene said. "You've just exacted revenge on behalf of your dearly-departed uncle. That's something special."

"My uncle . . . " I wiped snotty tears from my face. "He married me, you know. Me and Tonya. Out back behind his bait and tackle shop. And now . . . and now . . . "

"Yes, your uncle is dead, but you did not kill him."

Down on the floor, my uncle-demon let out an abrupt gurgle and kicked his right foot forward, then went limp again as blood streamed out of his mouth. I screamed and jumped in my seat. The 'dillo seemed unfazed. How many corpses had this animal been around in his life? Shit, better question: how many had it secretly been responsible for?

"Is he still alive?" I cried out.

The 'dillo shook his head, peering over the edge of the table. "Nah. He's dead as shit."

I tried to finish off the can of beer in front of me, but it was already empty. Refusing to look down at the floor, I got up and fetched another can from the fridge. Popped the tab and chugged the whole thing without turning around.

Then I got another. I poured a little of it on the flat surface of the table for Eugene to slurp, then took my time sipping the rest of it.

"I killed him," I said. "I really killed him. Oh god, what am I gonna do now?" I struggled to maintain my grasp on the beer. Then, to Eugene, I said, "You're telling me my uncle's real body is back at his bait and tackle shop? Like, we can go see it?"

Eugene made a movement like he was trying to shrug, except he didn't have any shoulders so it was really more up to the imagination than anything. "I'm no clairvoyant, Wayne. I cannot tell you where, exactly, this demon may have left your uncle's faceless body. I can only deduct based on what I know about your uncle, and that is very little other than what you've told me in passing. For instance, he's usually at the shop, correct? Seldom leaves?"

"Uh, as far as I know. He has a house next to it, too."

"So, then, based off that knowledge I think I could safely predict the general proximity of the body. I don't think the demon would have killed him and then taken the body very far. Demons aren't that careful. They're very sloppy creatures. I mean, case and point." He nodded at the corpse on the floor. "What exactly was his plan here? To just tackle us in the kitchen? Very embarrassing, if you ask me. Real amateur shit," the 'dillo said.

But something else was on my mind. "What am I gonna see if I cut off his face?"

"What are you going to see if you . . . oh, you mean *his* face?" Meaning the corpse in my kitchen.

"You said he was a demon, right? And that he removed my uncle's face and was wearing it like a mask. So what does his *real* face look like? That's what I want to know right now."

"What does it look like? Wayne, it looks demonic."

"I'm gonna find out," I said, not very confidently.

"Well, I can't wait to watch this," Eugene said, leaning over the edge of the table.

I pulled the knife out of the corpse's throat. It slid free smoother than I anticipated. Nearly fell back on my ass. I held up the blood-stained knife and examined my uncle-demon's face, trying to pinpoint the best spot to start cutting it off, then I reminded myself what exactly I was considering and decided maybe I was nowhere near drunk enough yet.

"You want another beer?" I asked Eugene.

And Eugene said, "Does an armadillo shit in the woods?"

I paused next to the fridge, debating the question he'd posed. "Um. I don't know. Do you?"

Again with the imaginary shrug. "I mean, I guess if I happen to be in the woods, sure. I'm no prude."

We each had another beer and talked more about demons and how they were intent on exterminating all armadillos from the planet. It all sounded pretty batshit to me, but consider the alternative: that this thing in my kitchen I'd stabbed in the throat wasn't a demon at all but in fact just my uncle. A person I had murdered. Judge me however you want but personally the demon theory sounded awfully preferable—so much so that I abandoned the idea of removing my uncle's face from his head and taking a gander at what was hiding behind it. Confirmation of the truth was a double-edged sword. It felt easier just to take the 'dillo's word for it. Did that make me lazy? A bad person? Would Tonya have had a lot to say about this decision? Well fuck her. She'd moved out. If she was still living with me, then there's a mighty good chance none of this shit would've happened in the first place.

"We do have to clean up the scene, though," Eugene said. "Maybe bury the body in the back yard, or something. Do you have a shovel?"

"Of course I got a shovel," I said. "Can't you dig holes, too? Isn't that like one of your . . . things?"

"Have you ever heard of an armadillo who could dig a grave, Wayne?"

"You're the only armadillo I've ever known."

"Well, no. I can't dig a grave," Eugene said. "Plus, if we're being honest here, I wasn't the one who killed him. That was all you."

I almost started crying again. "You told me to stand there with the knife!"

"Yeah, but I didn't tell you to let him run into it, for crying out loud. But that's okay. What happened is a good thing. This world is now one demon less than it was earlier this evening. But that doesn't mean you still aren't responsible for the consequences of your actions, Wayne."

There was something about the way he said my name that I found loathsome. Like he was better than me or something. Well, I could play that game, too. "Okay, *Eugene.*"

"Why did you just say my name like that?"

"Like what?"

"With such a bizarre emphasis."

"Takes one to know one—wouldn't you say, *Eugene*?" I asked.

"Takes what to know what, *Wayne*?"

The 'dillo sounded agitated. I couldn't decide if I liked him being annoyed or if I feared he would stop being my friend. I did not want to be alone right now. I did not want to be alone ever again.

"Okay," I said, defeated, "I'll go find the shovel."

I finished my beer, crushed the can, and tossed it in the trash.

At that exact moment of the can connecting with garbage, my doorbell went off, followed by a series of heavy, intimidating knocks.

"Now who the fuck is that?" the 'dillo asked.

My first thought was that it might be my uncle.

My *real* uncle, somehow having survived the demon's ambush.

But that raised a new fear. If my uncle *was* standing on the other side of the door, would he still have a face? According to Eugene, no, of course not, because that face was already in use with the corpse on my kitchen floor. So what would he look like, then? Like, exactly, what was I supposed to expect? A faceless man? What did that mean? Just . . . a skull, right? And he would still be well enough to come over here and ring my bell, knock on my door? Would he still be able to talk without a face? Would surgeons be able to reattach it, perhaps?

I opened the door with trembling hands, expecting to see a skull and instead finding a badge.

Officer Sebastian Plank had returned. This time, he already had his pistol out. "It's you," I said. "The wife-fucker."

He aimed his piece at me. "Sir, I'm gonna have to ask you to put down the knife."

"What fuckin' knife?" I asked, then realized I was still holding the knife I'd used to stab my uncle-demon. I dropped it at my feet. We both stared at it. The blade was red with blood, and so were my hands and the front of my shirt. I admit this didn't look great for me.

"Sir," Officer Sebastian said, "we've received multiple calls tonight reporting a disturbance at this address."

"What kind of goddamn disturbance."

He side-eyed the knife on the floor. "People screaming."

"There ain't been nobody screaming here. It's just me now," I said. "Which you, of all people, should know."

The cop raised his brow. "What is that supposed to—"

From the kitchen, my uncle-demon started screaming.

Then, also from the kitchen, Eugene shouted, "Oh, shit, this fucking guy is still alive! Wayne! Wayne, quick! He's still alive! Come finish killing him!"

I wondered if the cop had heard all of that. Judging by the look on his face, he did. Also, when I asked him if he happened to hear anything right then, he nodded like I was a fucking nutjob and said, "Yeah, of course I did," then

ordered me to get on the ground, which I obliged. Dickhead or not, the man had a gun and I hoped to avoid getting shot if at all possible. From everything I'd ever read or seen about gunshots, the one thing everyone made sure to get across was how painful it could be. Well, I'm sorry, but no thank you.

Sebastian headed into the kitchen. Slowly. I could tell he didn't really want to see what was going on in there. I didn't blame the cowardly piece of shit one bit. As someone who *did* know what was to be found in the kitchen, I wished like hell I could erase the imagery from my memory, that I could scrub it like shit stains from a toilet bowl.

Next to my head was the knife Sebastian had ordered me to drop. The dumb sumbitch had forgotten all about it—too distracted by the commotion from the kitchen. The way I saw it, I was left with two options here. Either I ignored the knife and remained on the floor, or I picked it up and continued the path I'd started the moment Tonya walked out of my life. I knew where option A would lead me: in a prison cell, on the news, disgraced and forgotten. Option B . . . well, that's when things got a bit less predictable. Less predictable and more . . . shit, well I'll just go ahead and say it: more *exciting*.

I grabbed the knife and got up.

Just in time to hear the cop scream from the kitchen.

The time to act was now, before it was too late, before he had a chance to comprehend the bizarre horrors he'd just stumbled into.

I charged into the kitchen, knife raised.

Eugene was now on my uncle-demon's chest, feasting upon the hole in his throat I'd previously created. Sebastian had his pistol raised at the animal and was yelling something about the 'dillo putting his hands up. I had just enough time to wonder if Sebastian had handcuffs small enough for Eugene before it was too late to think about anything other than stabbing him over and over in

the back, something I hadn't exactly planned on doing but, at the same time, hadn't I been secretly fantasizing about this very moment since Tonya informed me of this cocksucker's existence? Wasn't this what I wanted all along?

I did not stop stabbing him until the 'dillo said, "Bro, how long are you going to do that for?"

My arm was tired from all the stabbing. That kind of work, it takes a lot out of a fella. There was no way I had the energy to bury someone tonight. Make that *two* someones now. Things were far more complicated with the addition of Sebastian. There was a cop car in front of my house. Surely the police station was aware of his current location. After all, weren't they the ones who would've assigned him to this call in the first place? It was only a matter of time before backup arrived. And then what? As sad as it was to admit, I could only stab so many cops.

If I could only stab just one cop, yeah, I won't bullshit you: I was relieved this fuck had been the one. Sure, it might make Tonya sad, but given the circumstances my thirst for vengeance was more valuable than her romantic interests. He had shown up at my front door one too many times to rub my wife's adultery in my face. What did he expect to happen? For me *not* to stab him?

I wondered how long it'd take for Tonya to worry about her new lover's tardiness from work. When would she start getting concerned? Who would she call? Me? A sick part of me hoped so. I had no idea how I'd respond. Tell her the truth or play dumb? *Oh, baby, that's such a shame,* I might say, *I guess he wasn't the sorta man you hoped he was, after all.*

No. I didn't like thinking that way. Despite everything she'd done to me, Tonya was still my wife, right? Even if she no longer respected me, some stupid-ass part of me

still felt obligated to break the news to her myself. In a situation like this, either you were a man or you were a coward. I was sick of being the latter. I pulled out my phone and started scrolling for her name, then stopped. I took in the scene in my kitchen again. The reality of the situation I found myself in tonight. Was this really something I oughta talk about over the phone? For one thing, what if someone else was listening in? What a fool I'd be to admit to anything like over cellular communication. But also, this was real heavy shit. My uncle was a demon, yes, but as far as I knew Sebastian had only been a wife-thieving shithead. Still human, though. Still one of Tonya's many, many lovers.

I needed to break the news to her in person. This was going to devastate her. She would need someone to hug her and lie about everything being okay. I went through the cop's pockets until I found his wallet, then took out his ID and punched the listed address into my phone's GPS app.

"I'll be goddamned," I whispered. The miserable sumbitch lived not even five minutes away. Which meant all this time, Tonya had basically been within walking distance of the house.

"What's the plan here, exactly?" Eugene the armadillo asked me, having somehow helped himself to a new can of beer despite lacking opposable thumbs. At that point, I was past questioning the logistics of weird shit.

"We're going over to tell my wife what happened."

"We?"

"Yes. The both of us. She ain't ever gonna believe this shit if you don't show her you can really talk. She'll think I'm crazy."

"You know, Wayne, I don't talk just for anybody. They have to earn it."

I gave him a hard stare. "If you want to continue living in my house and drinking my beer and watching professional wrestling on *my* goddamn TV, then you're going to talk to her."

"Fair enough."

We got in my truck and took off. I left the bodies where they were in the kitchen. Same for the cop car in front of the house. Did I believe these problems would simply disappear in my absence? No, of course not. But was I secretly hoping they would? Shit—wouldn't you be?

I thought about buckling the 'dillo in the passenger seat, but truth be told I sorta enjoyed the idea of him getting flung forward during an abrupt stop. Nothing that would hurt him too much, of course. Maybe just irritate him a bit and give him a good scare. He seemed way too nonchalant regarding all the macabre activity that'd occurred in my house tonight. If he thought shit like this was going to be on regular rotation while living together then he was in for a rude awakening. Personally I was not a fan of any of this. Personally I would have preferred to be drunk on the couch watching TV and eating potato chips. I mean, hell, we could have just ordered a pizza. Instead I had to kill two people. Well, one person and one maybe-demon.

No. Definitely a demon. No maybe about it. It was too late to doubt the armadillo now. I had to put my utmost trust in his supernatural expertise. I mean his expertise in the supernatural. I wasn't trying to imply that his expertise was somehow supernatural, too. Although, I guess I wasn't too sure about that, either. It very well could have been.

Along the way, we did not listen to any music and we did not converse. We drove in silence. For a moment, I almost forgot the 'dillo could speak, and I was grateful for the lapse in memory.

As my phone's GPS app predicted, we reached my wife's lover's house within five minutes. It was a nice house, too. Goddammit the house was beautiful. I'm not ashamed enough to admit that. This was the house of a man who could afford several Amazon Echoes. A man who

could subscribe to all the streaming services and not bat an eye at the price hikes. All of this on a cop's salary, too? Pretty impressive. No wonder my wife had moved in. Shit, now that he was officially out of the picture, I couldn't help but wonder if I could join her here. Would she be cool about everything I was about to tell her, or would she be a total bitch and criticize me for accidentally committing homicide? When it came to Tonya, you could never really tell about these kinds of things.

Eugene followed closely behind me as I knocked on the door. It was late. I wasn't sure what time exactly, or how many hours had passed since bringing my uncle-demon home from his bait and tackle shop. I was feeling weird and discombobulated. I desperately wanted to lick the 'dillo again, but I didn't want to give him the satisfaction of knowing how much I enjoyed his juices. I realize that last sentence sounded disgusting. I dare any one of you to come up with a better way to phrase what I meant. Shit is not as easy as it looks.

Nobody answered the door. Not even after I rang the bell. I was sure Tonya was simply still asleep. She'd always been a difficult person to wake. Back when we were still together, I considered her heavy sleepiness kinky. But now? It was just a goddamn nuisance, is what it was. I was not impressed.

"Welp," Eugene said, crouched at my feet, "nobody can claim we didn't try, right?"

"I'm not giving up that easy," I said, and tried to open the door. Predictably, it was locked. The back door, on the other hand, was not. Well, okay, *technically* it was locked, but not after I busted open some glass with my elbow and reached through and unlatched the deadbolt. I froze and waited for an alarm to blare. The house remained quiet. I guess Officer Pipsqueak couldn't afford any security precautions after blowing his wad on artificial intelligence pods. It was a good goddamn thing the intruder was just me and Eugene and not somebody actually dangerous.

"Tonya!" I screamed, and realized I'd brought the kitchen knife with me. It was still covered in blood. Blood from my uncle-demon and blood from my wife's lover. "Tonya! I'm here!"

Eugene abandoned me and headed into the kitchen, surely in search for more beer. This armadillo was a bigger alcoholic than I was. If he was going to live with me, he'd need to find a way to chip in for groceries. I didn't expect him to get a job or anything, but perhaps he could learn to pickpocket.

"Tonya!" I shouted again. "It's me, your husband Wayne! I've come to deliver terrible news!"

Down the hallway, I heard some kind of activity. A hushed voice. I followed it to the last door on the left, then peeked my head through. Unable to adjust to the darkness, I flipped the light switch, revealing three small children huddled around a woman who was very much not my wife. She was holding up a knife very much like the one I'd brought with me. I wondered if we'd purchased them at the same store.

"Hey, you ain't Tonya," I said.

The children were crying. So was the woman.

"Dear god," she said, "please don't hurt my babies."

"I thought you were gonna be Tonya." I glanced around the room, trying to make sense of the situation. "You're not married to a cop named Sebastian by any chance, are you?"

One of the children cried out the word, "Daddy!"

I couldn't help it. I grinned. Hell, I did more than grin. I laughed. I laughed good and hard. This was delightful. This was delicious. All this time, and Tonya's new boytoy had himself a whole goddamn secret family? I couldn't wait to rub this in her face. She was going to be devastated, but in a funny way. Later I'd tell her about him being dead. First, the family. Hell, the being murdered part might even get me a thank you from her, after she found out what kind of despicable lowlife he really was.

I closed the bedroom door and went back out to the

living room and got my phone out and gave Tonya a call. As it rang, I examined myself in front of a mirror they had hung near the front door. Blood practically covered me from head to toe. No shit that family had been spooked. I looked fucking nuts. I started laughing even harder.

Then Tonya answered the phone. She sounded like I'd woken her up. "He-hello? Wayne?"

"Well if it isn't Tonya," I said, and hoped I sounded as badass as I thought I did.

"What do you want, Wayne? Goddammit, do you know what time—"

"I bet you're wondering where your lover Sebastian might be tonight."

"Sebastian?"

"Yeah. Aren't you curious why he isn't home from his shift yet, darling?"

Tonya waited a good ten seconds before she responded. "Um, Sebastian is home. I'm looking at him right now in bed with me. He's sound asleep."

I stopped smiling. "Well, now I know you're lying, because he's in my kitchen with a thousand knife wounds in his back. Along with my uncle. But not really my uncle. The demon who killed my uncle, I mean." None of this was coming out as I'd rehearsed in my head.

"He's what? Wayne, are you drunk?"

"Aren't you going to thank me?"

"Thank you for *what*?"

"He has a second family, you know. Your perfect little Sebastian. A wife, kids, you name it. I just saw them. They're ugly as shit."

"Wayne, if you call me again I'm gonna have to file a restraining order. Go to sleep."

She hung up the phone. I ignored her request and immediately redialed her number, but this time it went straight to voicemail.

What the hell had she been talking about, anyway? How could Sebastian be sleeping next to her? The

assumption was she'd lied to me, but for what reason? What did she have to gain by telling such a bizarre fib? The mind of my wife was an enigma, I tell you what.

Somewhere outside, I heard police sirens nearing.

I ran down the hallway and kicked open the door. The family screamed.

"You assholes! Did you really call the police on me?"

"Please don't hurt us!" the woman wailed. "Oh my god please leave us alone!"

"Fuck!" I slammed the door again and bolted through the house. "Eugene! We gotta go! They called the police!"

He didn't respond, but I remembered he'd gone to the kitchen, so I bee-lined in the direction any normal house would have their kitchen.

Just as I crossed the doorway threshold separating the living room from the kitchen, something round and pink shot out at my feet. The 'dillo. "Surprise, bitch!" he shouted, and it was too late to slow down. I tripped over his shell. I flew across the kitchen. And when I landed near the refrigerator, the knife I'd been carrying had somehow entered the side of my stomach. The blade had vanished inside me. All that was left was the handle.

"Ouchie," I gasped, rolling over onto my back. "Ouchie, ouchie, ouchie." I tried to pull the knife out of me, but the pain was too intense. I tried again for the hell of it and nearly passed out. I gave up on the idea of removing it. As far as I cared, the goddamn knife could live within me forever.

Across the kitchen, Eugene was laughing his ass off.

"Now why the hell did you go and do that?" I said. "That wasn't funny. That wasn't funny one goddamn bit."

"Maybe not to you," the 'dillo said. "But, from where I'm standing? Absolutely hilarious."

The police sirens sounded closer.

"C'mon, man, shit," I said. "We gotta get out of here."

"Oh, I'm for sure leaving. But you, on the other hand? I don't think so."

"What are you talking about?" My gut felt like it was

on fire. I couldn't make sense of anything the armadillo was saying.

"Tell me something, Wayne," he said, "did you really think we were friends? Even after I pissed on your shoe?"

"Huh?"

"My dude. You tried to shoot me with a shotgun. You got me drunk and tricked me into knocking myself out against a fire hydrant. You locked me in a cage like an animal. And you thought we were *friends*?" I never realized how evil an armadillo's laugh sounded until that moment. "How goddamn stupid are you, exactly? Wait. Don't answer that. You already did, when you immediately believed that bullshit about demons I fed you. Demons? Really, Wayne? In this day and age. No wonder Tonya left you."

"Hey now," I said, bleeding profusely from my stomach, "there's no reason to say anything we might regret."

The 'dillo stopped laughing. He stared at me and he sighed. I'd heard my wife sigh exactly the same way on the day she announced our separation. I didn't care for the noise one bit. "If you'd just let me continue on about my business," he said, "if you'd just been cool with me eating my bugs and digging my dirt, if you hadn't decided to push yourself into my life, then we would have been cool. Maybe we could have even become friends one day. If, like, we had met under more natural circumstances. But that isn't what happened, is it? Instead you had to trap me. You left me very little choice, Wayne. Now you are the one trapped—you poor, gullible man. Will you escape? Or will this be the conclusion of our lame will-they-or-won't-they Tom and Jerry charade? Be grateful the police are almost here. Pray they've brought an ambulance with them. Otherwise this really will be the end for you. If you make it through this maybe I'll come visit you in prison, assuming I can tunnel my way in. Do you think Tonya will do the same?"

"Fuck you," I said. "You fucking . . . you fucking 'dillo."

Eugene made an angry chittering noise. "Thanks for all the free beer, asshole," he said, then hopped through a doggy door leading to the back yard. Out of the house, and out of my life.

The police sirens were unbearably loud now. I tried to glance over the kitchen counter at the front door but the knife in my gut prevented any drastic movement. I did notice something peculiar on the counter, however. Something I'd only ever seen pictures of online before.

I leaned my head against the fridge and closed my eyes, listening to the approaching sirens. I wondered how long it'd take them to find the bodies back at my house, and how long after that for them to contact Tonya and inform her of my alleged crimes. I wondered what she would say. Would she be heartbroken? Would she be disappointed? Would she care at all?

I wondered if I'd ever hear from her again.

I wondered if armadillos really could talk.

I wondered a lot of things.

I thought about the object I glimpsed on Officer Sebastian Plank's kitchen counter. Suddenly it was all I could think about.

"Hey, Alexa," I moaned.

And the Amazon Echo on the counter said, "Yes? How can I help you today?"

But, in that moment, I couldn't think of a single question I wanted answered.

ACKNOWLEDGEMENTS

I first threatened to write this novella back in early 2020, after Alan Baxter released *The Roo* and several other writers joked about penning their own version featuring a murderous region-specific creature related to where each author resided. Since I live in San Antonio, armadillos seemed like the perfect choice for me. I wrote the first chapter and then promptly abandoned the project to work on other stuff.

From time to time, readers would ask me when I was going to release *The 'Dillo,* and I would give a range of answers from "Soon!" to "Never!" It wasn't until Chris K. and I started teasing the idea of launching the Ghoulish Ghosts imprint (merging his press Little Ghosts and my press Ghoulish Books) that I started seriously reconsidering writing it again.

So for these reasons, I must thank both Alan Baxter and Chris K. for indirectly and directly motivating me to write this thing. I think it turned out to be pretty entertaining, even if I gave Chris a mini heart attack with my schizophrenic writing practices.

Plus, how kickass is that cover art Chris whipped up?

I also must note that, going into this book, I knew pretty much nothing about armadillos, and I decided it would be funnier if this time I rejected my usual desire to bury myself in research. It is for this reason that I hope you, the reader, leave this novella somehow knowing less about armadillos than when you started.

Thanks for reading.
—Max Booth III

ABOUT THE AUTHOR

Max Booth III is a writer, publisher, editor, podcaster, and indie bookstore owner. They are the co-founder of Ghoulish Books, a publisher/bookstore hybrid specializing in horror. Born and raised in Northwest Indiana, they now live in San Antonio, TX

Find their work at www.TalesFromTheBooth.com